THE
ROYAL
WOODS

MATT
DUGGAN

KEY PORTER BOOKS

Library and Archives Canada Cataloguing in Publication

Duggan, Matt, 1957–
    The Royal Woods / Matt Duggan.

ISBN 978-1-55263-826-2 (bound) ISBN 978-1-55470-060-8 (pbk)

    I. Title.

PS8607.U376R69 2007   jC813'.6   C2006-906440-7

ONTARIO ARTS COUNCIL
CONSEIL DES ARTS DE L'ONTARIO

The publisher gratefully acknowledges the support of the Canada Council for the Arts and the Ontario Arts Council for its publishing program. We acknowledge the support of the Government of Ontario through the Ontario Media Development Corporation's Ontario Book Initiative.

We acknowledge the financial support of the Government of Canada through the Book Publishing Industry Development Program (BPIDP) for our publishing activities.

Key Porter Books Limited
Six Adelaide Street East, Tenth Floor
Toronto, Ontario
Canada M5C 1H6
www.keyporter.com

Text design and formatting: Marijke Friesen
Illustrations: Rebecca Buchanan

Printed and bound in Canada
08 09 10 11 12 5 4 3 2 1

I WROTE THIS STORY FOR MARY JUNE,
AND DID SO THANKS TO LISA AND CHESTER.

CHAPTER ONE

THE ROYAL WOODS

The place they now call The Royal Woods was once a farm. This place is on the great prairie, which is as flat as a pancake and as big as the biggest blue sky. But why is it called The Royal Woods? And what happened to the farm? To the north of the farm, a city grew and grew until it came to the very edge of the farm fields. When a city touches a farm, you know it won't be long before the farm is gone. And that's just what happened to this farm. First the cows went away, then the fences came down and the farm house stood empty, just watching the barn. Before long the house and barn were gone, too. Where does a farm go when the city comes along? Nobody knows. It just disappears, as if the cows ran away and the farm house and barn went chasing after them all across the long flat prairie.

Before you knew it, the farm was nothing but a memory and a big muddy field with a sign that read "The Royal Woods—Homes For Sale!" Then in came the builders with tractors and trucks, and soon there were roads, houses, a school and, of course, a shopping mall. This all happened so fast that if you didn't watch closely, you would have missed it. You could look one day and there would be the farm. When you looked the next day, the farm would be gone. The next time you happened to look, you would be so surprised by all the new houses and the school and the shopping mall and the freshly paved roads, you might think all these things had just dropped from the sky.

And that's exactly what red-haired Sydney thought when she first saw the place they called The Royal Woods. In fact, she said that very thing to her little brother Turk.

"Where did all this come from?" Sydney asked. "It's like it just dropped from the sky or something. And what happened to the farm?"

Not that Sydney expected an answer. How could Turk know where this place called The Royal Woods had come from, or where the farm had gone? Besides which, Turk wasn't much of a talker. He was so quiet that he would sometimes go for days without saying one single word. In fact, Turk was so quiet that Sydney often found she had to do his talking for him.

Sydney and Turk were peering out at The Royal Woods from behind some old black-bark trees that lined the banks of a little river. The river was called the Rat River. It was probably because of those very trees on the bank of the meandering little river that someone got the bright idea to name this new place The Royal Woods. Probably they'd thought that if they called it by what its name should really have been—The Rat River Woods, or The Missing Farm Woods—no one would want to live there, and they wouldn't be able to sell any of those brand new houses.

Before Sydney quite got over the shock of seeing The Royal Woods where the farm was supposed to be, she turned to look at the river behind her, just to make sure that it too hadn't disappeared while she wasn't watching. She was relieved to see the Rat River was still there, looking exactly as she remembered it. That's how Sydney knew that they were in the right place. She and Turk had been to the farm before, exactly two summers ago. And now they had come back, hoping to stay on the farm again, if only for a day or two, or maybe (Sydney secretly hoped) for longer. Maybe for much longer.

Earlier that morning they'd crossed a golf course and then followed the bank of the Rat River, walking on a narrow dirt trail that snaked through the trees, until they'd passed under a bridge that Sydney remembered. Further along, they'd come to a place that was even more familiar, where a big tree leaned out so far over the river that it looked like it could topple in at any second. And just as Sydney remembered, there was a tire swing tied to a limb of the big leaning tree, daring you to swing out and drop into the muddy little river below. Thrilled by her discovery of that tree—like seeing an old friend that hadn't changed one bit—Sydney took Turk by the hand and led him up the riverbank and out of the trees and into the field to find the farm.

And there it wasn't.

Red-haired Sydney was a tough-minded girl. She knew how things go in this world, and that you don't always get what you want. Sydney knew about all of this and more, because she'd had a good deal of experience of not getting what she wanted. But at that moment it felt somehow different, almost worse than her many other experiences of not getting what she wanted. Not only was she not getting what she wanted, but this time the thing that she wanted was not even there anymore. The farm was gone, and so she could never visit there again. It was also worse because they were so very far from their home, and it had been such a long hard journey to get there. The very sight of The Royal Woods crushed her with shock and disappointment.

"You sure this is the place?" Turk asked.

"Oh yeah," Sydney replied, "This is it all right. How many Rat Rivers are there? And that tree, the big bent one, we used to play on it. Remember?"

Turk remembered that tree very well. In fact, he remembered each and every small thing about that summer on the farm. Two years before, when he was six and Sydney was ten, they'd flown on a plane from the big city in the East where they lived, all the way out West to stay on the farm with their dad's old Uncle Frank and Aunt Lily. That was when their mother first got sick and had to go into the hospital. It was decided it would be best for Sydney and Turk to go stay out West for a while.

That summer on the farm had been so fine and sweet it almost (but not quite) made them stop worrying about their mom. That summer Sydney and Turk had done and seen a thousand things that they'd never done or seen before. Very early in the morning there were calves to pet, cows to milk, and ducks and chickens to feed. Then, after the big breakfast of pancakes and syrup that Aunt Lily always made, there was a tractor to ride on with Uncle Frank when he went out to mow hay in the fields. In the hot and lazy afternoons, there was the little river to play around, and that tire swing tied to the tree. They rode horses, fed wild deer, and caught catfish in the river. Best of all, there was their dad's Uncle Frank and Aunt Lily, who were old and kind, and who loved and cared for Sydney and Turk just like they were their very own children.

The only bad part about that summer was that it came to an end, which meant they had to say goodbye to Uncle Frank and Aunt Lily. Turk didn't like that part of the summer much at all. But Sydney promised him that some day, sooner rather than later, they'd come back to see Uncle Frank and Aunt Lily and stay on the farm again.

When they got back to their home in the big city in the East, Sydney and Turk often thought and talked about all the things they'd done and seen that long sunny summer on the farm. This was especially so because soon after they got home, their mother died. As you must know, there is nothing sadder in this big world than someone's mother dying. So it was only natural for Sydney and Turk to think and talk about times when they were happy, before they'd lost their mom. It seemed that the happiest time of all to think and talk about was that summer on the farm.

But thinking and talking about the farm was of no use now. They had dreamed and planned about coming to the farm for so long, and now that they had finally arrived, the farm wasn't even there. What most vexed Sydney about it was that she'd been given no warning.

"How come Dad never said anything about this? He could have at least told us where Uncle Frank and Aunt Lily went. Why didn't he at least tell us that much?"

Turk said nothing, knowing that Sydney would answer that question for herself.

"Because Dad never tells us anything, that's why," she said. "I give up."

With that, Sydney sat down on the ground, with her back turned to The Royal Woods, staring at the big bent-over tree by the river.

Turk didn't often see Sydney like this—sad and tired, sitting on the ground just staring at a tree. Sydney was always strong and brave and pushing straight ahead, and she always knew the thing to do next, no matter how big and difficult that thing was. But not this time, or not yet at least. Turk realized that Sydney had no idea what to do next because their one and only plan had been to get to the farm. And now there wasn't even a farm to get to, and Sydney had used up all of her strength. She had nothing left to make a new plan.

The worst thing Turk could have done at that moment would have been to ask Sydney what they were going to do now or, worse still, to whine and whimper. Turk knew it, so he didn't ask that question or start to whine and whimper. Instead, for a change, he just talked. He said whatever things came to his mind, just some nonsense words that he hoped might help Sydney feel a little better.

"I guess the cows got tired of sleeping in the barn and staying out in the field all the time," Turk said, looking out at the new houses and roads where the old farm used to be. "They must have moved into those houses. The cows are probably learning how to drive cars so they can go shopping in the mall and take their calves to school and all. And right now, I bet they're all just sitting around in their new houses, watching TV. You know what cows like to watch on TV?"

Sydney didn't answer.

"Mooooovies!"

It was a small and not very funny joke. But it made Sydney laugh anyway. At first she just smiled and looked away when Turk started talking about the cows in the houses. Then she snorted a little laugh, despite herself, when he talked about the cows driving to the mall. By the time Turk came to the punch line of his small and not very funny joke, Sydney was laughing so hard she had to hold her sides and lie on the ground to catch her breath. And then, to her surprise, Sydney found that she was crying at the same time as she was laughing. Crying and laughing at the same time is the kind of thing that can happen when you have a big problem and you're too tired to know what to do about it. And that's just how Sydney felt at that moment—like she was carrying a big problem on her back, and there was no place to put it down. When this sort of thing happens, it's a good thing to laugh and cry at the same time because after you're done, you usually feel a little bit better. So Turk was right about that.

But laughing and crying at the same time doesn't actually make the problem go away. So when Sydney was all finished with that, she sat up, wiped her tears away with a sigh, and asked the question that Turk had been careful not to ask. "What are we going to do now?"

"Get something to eat?" Turk suggested.

"Good idea," Sydney agreed. "I bet we can get something to eat at that stupid mall. Just look at that stupid mall. It's right where the barn used to be. What a stupid mall."

They picked up their backpacks and started for the stupid mall across a rough muddy field where Uncle Frank used to mow hay. With each step through the field, thick black mud stuck to the bottom of their shoes. The further they walked, the more the sticky muck collected on the bottom of their shoes. By the time they got to the mall parking lot, it was like they were wearing chocolate birthday cakes on their feet. But they walked right on across the sprawling parking lot, and it was only when they got to door of the mall that they paused. A big sign out front read, "The Royal Mall," and the mall was meant to look like a grand old fantasy castle, with pretend towers on all four corners and a fake moat gate at the front.

"Wait a minute. Look at you Turk," Sydney said. "You can't go into a mall looking like that, all filthy and dirty. You look like a little pig."

"Oink, oink," Turk said. "I'll just pretend I'm going into the barn. And anyway, look at you. Same deal."

Sydney examined her reflection in the sliding glass entrance door of the mall. Turk was right. She was just as dirty as he was, if not more so. It wasn't just the mud cakes stuck to the bottom of her running shoes that were of concern. From the top of her head to the tips of her toes, every inch of Sydney was covered with a layer of grease, dust and dirt so thick you'd have to scrape it off with a knife.

"Holy moly!" Sydney said, staring at her reflection. "Is that me?"

"Wave and see if it waves back," Turk suggested.

Sydney made a timid little wave, and sure enough, the filthy twelve-year-old red-headed girl staring at her from the glass door waved right back.

You might be wondering how Sydney and Turk managed to get so dirty. The reason why is that they travelled all the way there from the big city in the East by train. Obviously, you don't get that dirty by riding *inside* a train. But if, like Sydney and Turk, you ride on the *outside* of train, you will get very dirty indeed.

Riding on the outside of a train is not a very good idea. In fact, it's a very bad idea, and no one, especially young children, should ever even think about trying it. Sydney had gotten this bad idea from reading a book about a time when no one could find jobs, and men would hop on trains to travel from one place to another, looking for work. They called it "riding the rails," which was an expression she loved to say after she'd learned it. For Sydney, discovering this good but bad idea solved a problem she'd been pondering all winter long. She and Turk had secretly decided to visit Uncle Frank and Aunt Lily on the farm that coming summer. But the problem was, how would they get there? Sydney had saved enough money from babysitting for their food and other things, but she would never be able to make enough money for them to fly on a plane or to buy two train tickets. Or even bus tickets. So when she read about those men riding on trains for free, Sydney immediately thought that she and Turk could do the exact same thing. They would ride the rails.

You probably want to know how they managed to do this, and what their journey was like. The first thing to know is that Sydney can be a very determined girl, so when she gets an idea in her head, no matter how bad that idea might be, she will almost certainly make that idea happen. In order to make *this* bad idea happen, Sydney learned everything she could about trains and where they go. That was surprisingly easy to do because, as it turns out, train tracks pretty much only go north and south, or east and west. All Sydney had to do was find the track that went east and west, and then figure out when the trains travelling west passed by.

So very late one night, exactly one day after the last day of school for summer holidays, Sydney and Turk tiptoed out of their house and made their way to the train track that went east and west. They had been planning and talking about this for months, so by then everything was ready. In their backpacks they each carried one change of clothes, some soap, toothpaste and a toothbrush, six peanut butter and honey sandwiches, a thermos full of chocolate milk, and six apples. They also had a flashlight, some matches to start a campfire with, and a map of the country in case they got lost.

Just before they got to the train tracks, Sydney stopped and faced Turk. "We have to hereby solemnly swear that we won't turn back or even talk about home, no matter what."

"Swear," Turk said.

Then they did their secret handshake—two snaps, two slaps, and one long palm slide.

They climbed the fence at a place where Sydney knew the trains passed by very slowly. Then they sat and waited. Just when the sun was coming up that morning, and the sky was changing from black to blue, the big westbound freight train came by, right on schedule. All they had to do was walk along beside it and climb onto a train hitch between two boxcars.

This turned out to be a much more difficult and frightening thing to do than Sydney had anticipated. Trains, even slow-moving trains, are seriously big and powerful machines that can squash a twelve-year-old girl and her eight-year-old brother just as quick as a wink. But Sydney ignored her fear and went straight ahead. She gritted her teeth and took Turk by the hand, and together they jogged along beside the rumbling freight train.

"Come on!" Sydney yelled, trying to be heard above the screaming and squeaking metal wheels of the train and the banging and clanging of the boxcars.

And then they did it. With a quick push to help him, Sydney launched Turk onto the train hitch and scrambled up behind him. Once they got onto the train, they wiggled around till they were sitting comfortably facing each other across the hitch between two boxcars. When they looked at each other and realized that they'd made it, that they were actually on the train, and that it was actually moving—well, what do you think they did then? They laughed like mad of course. Just seeing each other's face, all lit up with excitement and already smudged with grease and dirt made them howl with laughter.

From reading that book about the men riding the rails, Sydney had gotten the idea that they could easily move about on the outside of the train and find a nice open boxcar to ride inside. Maybe they could even find a half-empty cattle car, where they could pile up some straw to make a cozy bed, and even start a little campfire in case it got cold. But unfortunately, it wasn't like that at all. As the train pulled through and then out of the city, it moved faster and faster, until the track ties beneath their feet flew by so quickly that it made them dizzy just to look down. And all the things of the city—the buildings and trees, the cars and the people—flashed by on both sides, faster and faster. Riding on that train was like hanging onto a big metal monster, a big roaring metal monster, a monster that didn't care about anything and could not be controlled or stopped by anyone. All that Sydney and Turk could do was hold on tight and hope that all this would soon be over.

Time does funny things when you're doing something difficult. If, for example, you find yourself holding on for dear life to a fast-moving train, you would be surprised to find how slowly time passes. Sydney knew from her research that it took this train twenty-four hours to travel from the big city in the east to the first city you come to in the prairies, which is where they planned to hop off. But those twenty-four hours felt more like twenty-four days. Every minute felt like an hour. Not only could they not move about on the outside of the train to find a nice half-empty cattle car to make a cozy bed of straw for lying down, they could not even talk over the roaring engine and screaming wheels, and they could not even sleep or eat because they had to stay awake and hang on with all their might so as not to fall off. All they could do was sit tight and watch the world fly by.

For the first part of the day they passed through farm country and the backs of small towns. After it turned dark, they travelled through the black night, with the world's biggest lake on one side of them and the world's biggest forest on the other. The train honked and roared and rattled and squealed as it rolled up and around big hill turns and plunged down into dark forested valleys. And it was cold too, with the water of mighty Lake Superior letting go of its long winter chill.

You can probably imagine how relieved and happy Sydney and Turk felt when the first hint of morning light revealed that the train was now out on the warm open prairie. The track went perfectly straight, and all around them was sky and flat land, as far as the eye could see. It wasn't long before the train came to a stop in a sprawling rail yard. From studying her map, Sydney knew that they had arrived in the city just north of the farm. All they had to do now was walk out of the rail yard and head west until they came to the Rat River. From there they'd turn left and follow the river south until they found the farm.

The only problem with that plan was they were so dizzy and half-crazy with fatigue from hanging onto that train all day and all night that at first, they couldn't even walk. Turk didn't think he'd ever be able to walk again. When he climbed down off the train and stood on the gravel beside the train tracks, it felt like the entire world was rocking and swaying beneath his feet. He tried to walk, but all he could do was stagger around for a few steps before falling to the ground. Two more attempts at walking ended with the same results. The third time he fell down, Turk just lay there.

"You okay?" Sydney asked, gripping a pole beside the tracks so that she too wouldn't fall over. "We made it! We're here, Turk!" she added, her voice weak and croaking but trying to sound enthusiastic.

That's when Turk realized that not only could he not walk, he couldn't hear anything either. Twenty-four hours of banging clanging train noise and clatter had planted a loud ringing roar deep inside his head. He feared that he'd never be able to walk or hear again. When Sydney spoke to him, all Turk could hear was, "Wa wa wa wa? Waa wa wa! Wa wa Turk!"

It's amazing what six peanut butter and honey sandwiches and a thermos of chocolate milk can do for you. Right there on the gravel beside the train tracks, Sydney got Turk to sit up and she fed him some food from their backpacks. The sandwiches were all squashed and the chocolate milk was warm, but Turk had never tasted anything so good. Sydney ate and drank too, and when they were finished, they both felt strong enough to be on their way.

You already know what happened after that. They did find the Rat River, but unfortunately there was no farm to be found.

It had taken them all day to walk from the train yard, and now there they were, standing outside the mall where the barn used to be, starving hungry and so dirty that Sydney said, "We've got dirt on our dirt. I don't think we'll ever get clean again."

Out of peanut butter and honey sandwiches, and too dirty to go into the mall to buy something to eat, it was Turk's turn to have a very good but bad idea.

"You know what we should do?" he asked.

Sydney shook her head. "No. What?"

Turk pointed across the parking lot at a gas bar and car wash. "We should go over there and clean up."

"We're way too dirty to clean up in a washroom," Sydney said. "We need more than just a sink to get this off."

"Not the washroom," Turk said. "We'll go through the car wash."

Sydney needed only two seconds to consider this idea before saying, "Now that is a very great idea."

CHAPTER TWO

THE SHACK BY THE RIVER

W e'd like to use the car wash, please," Sydney said to the man in the booth at the gas bar.

It's a good thing for Sydney and Turk that the man in the booth, whose name was Kumar, had only recently arrived from India. Because he was new to the country, Kumar was still learning the ways of the local people. So when he saw these two amazingly dirty children looking up at him through the window of the gas bar booth, he thought that getting amazingly dirty was something that children here must do just for fun. In any case, he was far too polite to ask them how they had gotten so amazingly dirty. Kumar studied Sydney and Turk through a pair of black-frame glasses. He was a thin young man with a warm smiling face, and he seemed very pleased and proud to be wearing his sparkling bright orange and white gas bar uniform. Sydney was struck by how remarkably handsome Kumar looked.

"But, where is your car, miss?" Kumar asked.

"Our dad's over at the mall with the car," Sydney replied. "He'll be here in a minute."

"I see," Kumar said. "Well then! Would you prefer the Super-Duper Wash Special?"

"Um. Yeah. Yes, please," Sydney answered.

"Very good," Kumar said, pressing some buttons inside the booth.

"Would you be interested in having the Under Car Jet Water Blaster, miss?" Kumar asked.

"What does that do?" Sydney asked.

"It's for cleaning under the car, miss. It will make every-thing under the car just as clean as new," Kumar answered.

Sydney glanced at Turk and noted how dirty his shoes and pants were. "Yes please," she said.

Kumar pressed some more buttons inside the booth. Turk, who was following this discussion very closely, was beginning to have serious doubts about his great idea.

"Would you prefer the Extra Super Soapy Wash?" Kumar said.

"Oh, yes, please," Sydney said.

"Excellent!" Kumar said as he pressed some more buttons.

"Super Scrubbing Action?" Kumar asked.

"Yep, that too," Sydney replied.

"Very well then," Kumar said, pressing some more but-tons. "And finally, would you be wanting the Deluxe Super

Hot Lime Wax Treatment today?"

Turk was appalled to see that Sydney was seriously considering this question.

"Hmmmm. . . . Wax, eh? . . ." Sydney said, thinking it over.

"Wait a minute! Sydney, are you nuts?" Turk said to her. He turned to Kumar, "No sir, we will not be needing the Deluxe Super Hot Lime Wax Treatment today, thank you."

"As you wish," Kumar said. "That will be seven dollars and thirty-five cents, please."

Sydney pulled out the money from her backpack and paid him.

"The car wash is all set," Kumar said. "Just press the button when your father arrives with the car."

"Thank you!" Sydney sang.

Sydney and Turk crossed the lot from the booth to the car wash. They dropped their backpacks and peered into the long narrow building with its various cleaning devices and machines. It was pretty easy to figure out what most of these things did, even when they were just sitting in the dark, quietly waiting for the next car to wash. There were big round scrub brushes on both sides, long squiggly rubber strips hanging down from the ceiling, and huge water sprayers poking out from everywhere.

All of these devices and machines looked much bigger and more menacing than Turk had anticipated, and by now he was dearly wishing that he'd kept his great idea to himself. "On second thought," Turk said quietly, "maybe this isn't such a great idea."

Sydney looked over at Turk, her eyes wide with excitement. She hadn't heard a word he'd said. "This is going to be so much fun!" Sydney said. "I guess we just press the button and hop on and ride those two belts on the floor. They'll pull us right through, just like we're cars. This is going to be so cool!"

Turk wasn't convinced that this was going to be either fun or cool, and he watched in horror as his sister stepped toward a big red button on the wall.

"Get ready! After I press the button, hop on the belt. It's going to be loud though, so cover your ears and keep your eyes closed and your mouth shut!"

"How about if we? What if we? I think maybe we should . . ." Turk stammered, trying to delay Sydney while he thought of some other way that they could get cleaned up. "Hey! I know! Why don't we go wash in the river?" he croaked in desperation.

"Are you kidding? That river's pure mud. All set?" And with that, Sydney pressed the button and the car wash sprang to life with a gush of water and a roar like a jet airplane taking off.

"Hop on!" Sydney yelled, as she pushed her terrified little brother onto the moving belt on the floor.

You've probably been inside a car when it goes through a car wash, and so you know what that's like. But what you probably don't know is what it's like to be on the *outside* of the car. However, if you have a good imagination, you would be able to guess that it isn't a very relaxing experience.

The first thing that happened was that Turk and Sydney were blasted all over with water. Water came at them from everywhere, all at once—up, down, and both sides. The Under Car Jet Water Blaster not only cleaned the mud and grime from their shoes and pants, it almost tore them right off. Turk feared that it was going to shoot them straight through the roof.

After they'd passed through the water spray, they had a few brief seconds to catch their breath before the belt carried them into the next phase of the car wash. Turk looked over at Sydney and wasn't surprised to see that she was limp with laughter, just like she was enjoying a thrilling ride at the Exhibition. Turk also tried to laugh, hoping that it would help him to relax and enjoy the ride too, but the only sound that came out of his mouth was a tiny little mouse squeak.

Then it was time for the soap. The long rubber strips dropped down on them from above, shaking from side to side like a thousand angry snakes, drenching them in bubbling soap suds. It was at this point that Turk wondered why Sydney had felt it necessary to request the Extra Super Soapy Wash. He held his breath and kept his eyes tightly shut. It was a struggle just to stay standing up under the weight of all those tons of soapy suds dumping down on him.

But the worst part of all, Sydney and Turk agreed later, were the scrub brush rollers. When they talked about it the next day, Sydney actually apologized for having asked for the Super Scrubbing Action, and she agreed with Turk that it was much more scrubbing action than they actually needed.

After they passed the scrub brushes, the soap was rinsed off in a cold shower that felt like they were passing under Niagara Falls. Finally, there was a blast of hot air, like a howling desert windstorm, that left them bone-dry.

When the whole thing was over and the machines all fell silent, they staggered out into the bright sunshine on the far side of the car wash. Their hair stood straight up on their heads, their mouths hung open, and their eyes were wide with shock. They were completely clean however, perhaps cleaner than they'd ever been in their entire lives.

"Well," said Turk, "please remind me to never do that supposedly fun thing again."

"Yes, and please remind me to never permit you to do that supposedly fun thing again."

It was Kumar, standing right there beside them with his arms crossed, his crisp orange and white uniform dazzling bright in the sun. "Now I see why you chose not to request the Deluxe Super Hot Lime Wax Treatment, and thank goodness for that."

At first, Kumar was very angry with them. He wanted to know where their father was with the car, and why they had done such a naughty and dangerous thing. Furthermore, he would like to know how they had gotten so dirty in the first place, and he demanded to speak with their father about all of these things.

"I have two children of my own, back in my home country. It makes a terrible pain inside my heart just to think of them behaving in such a ridiculous and foolhardy manner. Even stupid, if I can be forgiven for saying so," said Kumar.

As usual, Sydney did the talking. She explained that they had gotten dirty playing in the river, and that their father would be so angry they were afraid to go home like that. She apologized for using the car wash when they didn't even have a car, and she promised that they would never do it again.

"All very well, miss," Kumar said. "But still I insist on discussing the matter with your father. You seem like very good and polite children, and very well brought up, I am suspecting. I am certain that your father would not be wanting you to use this car wash for your daily cleaning purposes. I want very much to discuss these matters with your father."

"Okay," Sydney said. "We'll just go to the mall and phone him. We'll be right back. But meanwhile, sir, please accept our most sincere apologies for any distress this might have caused you. I'm certain that your own children would never behave in such a foolhardy, and—you are right to say so—stupid manner."

Kumar softened when Sydney said that. He smiled and told them that when he spoke with their father, he would try to avoid getting them into trouble. He would mention what polite children they were, and say that it all must have been a dreadful mistake.

Then the three of them shook hands and introduced themselves by name. After which Sydney and Turk collected their backpacks and set off for the mall, feeling more hungry than ever, but also pleased that they were finally clean, even though it had been such an ordeal to get that way.

"But how are we going to bring Dad back to talk with Kumar?" Turk asked as they walked across the parking lot.

"Well, to be honest Turk, we're not. We're never going to see Kumar again anyway," Sydney said.

Turk didn't like that at all. Kumar had been pretty nice to them, and Turk didn't like the idea of disappointing him. Even though her brother didn't say anything about it, Sydney knew exactly what he was thinking.

"Don't worry, it's just a little candy lie. Sometimes you have to give out little candy lies when you need to smooth things over and keep people happy," Sydney explained.

"How did you get so good at giving out little candy lies?" Turk asked. "You even had me believing you back there."

"I don't know. Practice I guess. Sometimes I even believe them myself."

"Really? From now on I'm going to tell you when that happens."

<hr />

At the very centre of The Royal Mall, Sydney and Turk found the usual food court which served all the usual food served in all the places usually found in shopping mall food courts. There was a Mama Mia Meat Beat Ball Frenzy, a Super Happy Chicken Factory, a Porky Pie Pork Pies, a

Block Long Toasted Sandwich Pit, and of course, a Mad Scottish Clown Burger.

"It's all your old favourites, Turk," Sydney said. "Total rubbish. But what are you going to do? Choose your poison."

"Pizza," Turk said. He was too hungry to say even one more word.

After they'd finished eating, they wandered around the mall while Sydney tried to think of a way to solve their next big problem—where were they supposed to sleep after it got dark? They had gotten up before dawn the day before, and hadn't slept a wink while riding on that train overnight, and now that they were full of food, they were feeling very sleepy indeed. But try as she might, no good ideas came into Sydney's head, probably because she was too tired to think. They sat on a bench beside a gushing fountain in the mall, watching all the people walk by. All Sydney could think about was how everyone there had a home to go to and a nice bed to sleep in. Everyone except for them.

"I wonder if Uncle Frank and Aunt Lily ever come shopping here," Turk said. "Maybe if we just sit here we'll see them. Eventually."

"I highly doubt it," Sydney said.

"Well, how in the heck are we supposed to find them then?" Turk asked.

Sydney didn't have an answer for that. If she said what she really thought—that it would be next to impossible to find Uncle Frank and Aunt Lily now—Turk would no doubt ask why they shouldn't just turn around and go straight home right then and there. And Sydney was fully determined to never go home again. In truth, Sydney would have run away from home even if she had known that the farm was gone and they had no place to go. Turk, on the other hand, had only made this journey so that he could visit Uncle Frank and Aunt Lily on the farm.

"Don't worry. We'll find them. Promise," Sydney said finally. At first, she thought of this as just another little candy lie, one meant to smooth things over with Turk and keep him happy. As soon as she said it though, Sydney realized that it wasn't really a little candy lie at all. It was more like a dirty trick she was playing on Turk, and that gave her a terrible feeling. But it seemed to her that, for now at least, she had no choice.

"We just need some time here to look around for them. Wait and see, we'll find them somehow. For now though, we've just got to take things day by day, and deal with everything as it comes," Sydney said, wanting to change the subject. "Beginning with—where are we going to sleep tonight?"

Sydney was relieved when Turk said he might have an idea. "Let's go out back behind the mall, where they put the garbage," Turk said. "I bet we can find some cardboard boxes and stuff. And then we can make a house by the river."

Sydney couldn't decide if that was a good idea or not, but it was the only idea they had, so she thought they might as well give it a try.

The sun was a magnificent flaming orange ball dropping into the prairie out past the parking lot as they walked around behind the mall to where the garbage dumpsters were kept. Just as Turk had predicted, there were stacks of cardboard boxes there, all neatly piled up and waiting to be carried away. All they had to do was find a couple of nice big boxes suitable for making a house, and then they could be on their way. The only problem was, there was someone else there, and he seemed to have the same idea.

On the far side of the dumpsters was a crazy man loading a shopping cart. He was tall and lanky, with a long orange beard and a head of mad scraggly hair. Under a canary yellow tuxedo jacket, he wore at least five shirts, each one a different and brilliant colour. He had a red running shoe on one foot, and a blue cowboy boot on the other. Around his neck he wore a bicycle chain with a giant alarm clock tied to it, and he had ladies' white satin gloves on his hands. His voice sounded like a chain being dragged down a gravel road, and while he worked loading his shopping cart, he talked and sang and whistled. Most of all, he whistled. Every few seconds he'd start to whistle, almost as though he couldn't help but whistle. He whistled the most beautiful and exotic bird songs that Sydney and Turk had ever heard. It sounded just like real birds, so much so that at first Turk looked around to see where all the birds were, before realizing that it was actually the shopping-cart man doing the whistling. Each time the man whistled, it was a different bird song, and each song was more sweet and pure than the one before.

Sydney and Turk were peeking at the man from behind a dumpster some distance away. It's rude to stare and laugh at someone just because they're different, but in this case, it was impossible not to stare and laugh. This guy was amazing. They covered their mouths with their hands and tried to look away, but they couldn't help themselves.

When they finally managed to stop spying on him, Sydney said, "Let's go find a good spot by the river. We'll come back for some boxes when that crazy bird man is finished loading up his shopping cart."

———

Sydney and Turk didn't need to cross through the muddy field to get back to the riverbank. They knew a better route. Behind the mall at the end of the parking lot, they found the trail they used to use to get down to the river from the farmhouse. It led them right back to the big bent-over tree on the riverbank. Sydney suggested that they walk a little further on, and try to find a good flat place to build their cardboard house. All Turk could do was yawn and nod his head in agreement.

They followed the trail along the river for a bit, but they didn't get far before Turk plunked himself down right where he was, too spent to take even one more step.

"Come on Turk, don't quit on me now. Just a little further up, and for sure we'll find the perfect place," Sydney urged.

"Okay," Turk said, "let's get going." And with that, he rolled over, curled up on the ground and fell fast asleep.

"Oh no. Not here," Sydney said desperately. "What am

I supposed to now?"

The light was slowly fading on the riverbank, and Sydney looked all around, hoping that she could see some place where they might possibly sleep for the night. That's when she noticed something shiny a little way off the trail.

Sydney went to investigate, leaving Turk for the moment asleep on the trail. She climbed up the riverbank and came to a clearing in the trees. The shiny thing that caught her eye was a hubcap from a car. It was just one of a thousand bits and pieces that someone had carefully assembled to make a small but solid house. The walls of the house were made from of all sorts of things—car parts, scraps of wood, sandbags from flood dykes, and broken patio stones. The roof was mostly made from leafy tree branches, but there were many other bits and pieces too, including umbrellas and even a Ping-Pong table. The entrance to the little house was an old car door. Sydney peaked through the window of the car door and, to her amazement, there was a neatly made bed, complete with blankets and a pillow.

The one and only thing in Sydney's mind at that point was to find somewhere for Turk to sleep. She didn't care about whose place this was, or if they would mind if Sydney and Turk used it, or even if they might be coming there that very night. All she knew was that Turk was already sleeping, and that she had to find a proper place for him to lie down. She couldn't believe her good fortune in having discovered a real bed, all made up and ready, right there on the bank of the Rat River.

It was a struggle to get Turk up on his feet and headed in the direction of the little house. But Sydney coaxed and half carried him, and Turk stumbled and sleepwalked up the riverbank and into the clearing. Sydney pulled the car door open, and Turk tumbled inside and plunged straight into bed. She pulled his backpack off his shoulders and tucked him in under the covers. Turk fell into the deepest sleep he'd ever known.

Sydney went back outside and sat on a stump. Of course, she was just as tired as Turk. But strange to say, she didn't feel much like sleeping just then. Maybe it was because she was too tired to sleep, or maybe it was because she was beginning to worry if staying there had actually been such a good idea. What if the person or persons who owned the house came along? Would they be mad at them for using it? Maybe they should have hidden out in the mall and tried to find a place to sleep in there. Well, there was nothing she could do about it now. Not even a shot from a cannon would wake up Turk.

After she was done worrying about all that, she began to worry about Turk. She got up and peeked through the car door window and watched him sleeping. He looked like a little baby lying there, and Sydney was reminded of the fact that Turk was only eight years old, and that it was her job to take care of him. She began to feel quite bad about all the hardships their journey had put him through—that crazy train ride, the long hike from the rail yard, at the end of which there was no farm and no Uncle Frank and Aunt Lily to greet them. And then getting cleaned up in a car wash, and eating dinner at the mall, and after all of that, they had no place to stay. Turk had been through so much, and yet he hadn't complained, not even once. Turk had always thought of his big sister as the bolder and braver of the two of them, but sitting there by herself, Sydney realized that it was really Turk who had the most courage. The only reason that she could be so brave was because Turk was even braver. It was Turk that made Sydney strong, and without him by her side, she wouldn't be able to do much of anything.

Right then and there Sydney decided that she had to take better care of Turk, beginning with finding a proper place to stay. They didn't have enough money to travel any further or to go into the city and get a motel room. So they'd need to find some place to live there, in The Royal Woods. But where?

Then it came to her all at once. This was Sydney's Great Big Idea, and it came to her like a gift from heaven. She suddenly knew exactly how she and Turk would find a place to stay. It made her smile all to herself just to sit and ponder this fresh and amazingly wonderful idea. She turned it over and over in her mind, and the idea just kept getting grander and more magnificently perfect.

While Sydney was thinking these thoughts, all alone in the quiet dark, she became aware of a sound. It was a very strange sound, unlike anything she'd ever heard before, and it seemed to be getting louder and coming her way. Sydney listened hard.

It sounded very much like a big whistling bird pushing a shopping cart down the trail beside the Rat River.

CHAPTER THREE

THE MAN WHO COULDN'T NOT WHISTLE

ey there, Red! How's it going?"

It was the crazy bird man they'd seen behind the mall, calling out to Sydney like she was his old long lost best friend as he pushed his shopping cart into the clearing.

Sydney's heart was thumping in her chest, and she had to force herself to breathe in and out. She felt an urgent impulse to scream, jump up, and run like mad. (Which, by the way, is exactly the right thing to do whenever you are truly afraid of someone.) But she had to use every ounce of her willpower to resist this urge to flee. With Turk dead asleep in the little house, Sydney had no choice but to hold still and wait to see what would happen next. She sat frozen to the stump, watching the bird man's every move.

The man whistled and sang a cowboy song as he steered his shopping cart onto a sheet of plywood lying beside the house, just like he was parking a car in his driveway. He took the cardboard out of the cart and stacked it in a tidy pile.

"Where's the little guy?" the bird man asked in his gravel road voice.

Sydney opened her mouth to answer, but no words came out.

"Sleeping inside, I bet. Well, that's just nifty," the man growled, and then went back to work. "It's dinnertime for the mosquitoes, so we'd better get a fire going there, Red," the man said, after he'd finished emptying the cart.

Mortified, Sydney watched as he gathered an armful of sticks from a pile beside his house, all the while whistling bird songs.

"It's Sydney."

Sydney was so amazed that she was able to talk that she hardly recognized her own voice.

"Beg your pardon?" the man said.

"My name. It's not Red. It's Sydney."

The one thing Sydney could not stand was being called "Red," or any other name that called attention to the colour of her hair. Like many red-headed girls, Sydney had always hated her hair, even though red is the most rare and beautiful hair colour of all.

"Sydney, eh? Okay then, Syd it is. But you shouldn't take

any notice of someone calling you names, Syd. It just inspires them to think of even worse names. People call me names all the time, and I don't care a whistle. And hey—I will bet you one Hawaiian doughnut that you were calling me some excellent names back there by the dumpsters, when you and the little guy were spying and laughing at me."

"That wasn't us! We never spied on you or laughed or called you names!" Sydney sputtered in indignation.

"No, eh? Must've been some evil little kids who look just exactly like you then. But I'll give you this much. At least you don't throw things. I don't mind the spying, or the laughing, or the name-calling. But when they get bored with that, some members of the public decide it's time to start throwing things. And I'll tell you what, I don't like that very much at all. So thank you kindly for not throwing things at me. I genuinely appreciate it."

While he talked, the bird man was carefully arranging sticks in a tiny firepit made from bits of broken sidewalk. His every move was quick and nimble, and Sydney noticed the delicate way he touched things with his clean white satin gloves. When the sticks were all arrayed in a small perfect pyramid, he reached into the pocket of his yellow tuxedo jacket and pulled out a shiny chrome barbecue lighter. With one touch of the lighter, the fire started.

"Shep McParlain," the man said, holding out his hand for Sydney to shake.

"Glad to meet you," Sydney said, lightly touching his silk gloved hand.

"Pull up by the fire there, Syd. It'll keep the mosquitoes off, unless you feel like feeding them," Shep said as he slid up a stump and sat down across the fire from Sydney.

He was right—the mosquitoes were beginning to buzz and bite. Sydney moved a little closer to the fire, just inside the veil of hazy smoke where the mosquitoes wouldn't enter. She was still too afraid of the man to look at him directly, so Sydney kept her eyes on the fire. But she couldn't resist stealing the occasional peek at the outrageous clothes he was wearing, and each time she peeked, she noticed some other strange and wonderful detail. She guessed, correctly as it turned out, that there was a reason for each and every thing he wore and carried, and after a while of sitting there listening to him whistle, she simply had to ask him a question or two. She also figured if she could get him talking, maybe the bird man would forget about going to bed, and they could stay up conversing till dawn. In that way, her little brother might enjoy a full night's sleep. It would only involve about ten to twelve hours of steady talking, Sydney calculated.

"Sir?" Sydney began cautiously.

Shep stopped whistling.

"That's just about the worse name of all you can call me, Syd. My name's Shep, remember? Shep McParlain Junior, actually. It's my father's name. He was half German Shepherd, half Irish Setter, God rest his soul."

"Okay, um. Shep? I hope you don't mind if I ask you but . . . well . . . why are you wearing one red running shoe and one blue cowboy boot?" Sydney asked.

"Because I like red and blue, that's why. I also like green, yellow, purple, mauve, peach, and paisley," Shep replied, sensibly.

"Yes, but I mean, why one boot and one running shoe? Isn't that sort of, you know, a little bit awkward?" asked Sydney.

"Can be, at times. Very awkward, now that you mention it. But you see, the boot's for dancing, putting out fires, and horseback riding. And the sneaker's for sporting events, puddle jumping, and tree climbing. Not to mention fleeing the scene. You gotta be ready for pretty much anything around here."

That answer seemed reasonable enough to Sydney. But maybe it only seemed reasonable because she hadn't slept in two days, and now here she was sitting beside a house made from car parts and things salvaged out of the garbage, on the bank of the Rat River where the farm was supposed to be, talking to a man in a yellow tuxedo jacket with an alarm clock around his neck. Maybe any answer would have seemed reasonable to Sydney just then. She would have liked to ask Shep more questions about what he was wearing, but as soon as he stopped talking, he started whistling. So Sydney decided to ask him about that instead.

"Um . . . Shep?"

"How can I help you, Syd?"

"I hope you don't mind if I ask you but, why do you whistle so much?"

"Good question," Shep replied. "Simply put, it's because I can't *not* whistle. Fact is, I'm not even the one who's doing the whistling. It comes from someplace else and just passes right through me, whether I want it to or not. The minute I stop talking, here comes the whistling. And truth be told, all this whistling has caused me nothing but trouble."

"Really? What kind of trouble?" Sydney asked, genuinely curious.

"Employment trouble for one. I always get fired from jobs for excessive whistling. I've been an astronaut, accountant and an actor, a baker, banker and a barber, a cook, cleaner and a cosmetologist, a doctor, driver and a dentist, an engineer, electrician and an excavator, a fireman, philosopher and a used car salesman. And I got fired from each and every one of those jobs for excessive whistling. If I could find a job where all I had to do was talk, there wouldn't be any problem. You see, if I was talking all the time, I wouldn't start in with the whistling."

Sydney pondered his problem for a moment. "Have you ever thought about being a teacher? They never stop talking," she pointed out.

Shep was impressed by the suggestion. He raised his eyebrows and frowned, thinking it over. "Now there's an idea. I never even thought of that. I certainly got the wardrobe for the job, which is half the battle in any employment scenario. Why? They looking to hire teachers at your school?"

A picture of Shep McParlain, standing in front of her grade seven class at school, popped into Sydney's head. She had to look away and slap her hand across her mouth to prevent herself from busting up laughing.

"I'll take that as a no," Shep said, only mildly annoyed.

Shep put some more sticks on the fire and blew on the flame. It rose up crackling and snapping, and Sydney sat staring into the fire as though hypnotized. She no longer felt frightened by Shep, and it was soothing just to sit still after all the stress and strain of the past two days. Shep's whistling became soft and quiet, like a gentle little night bird. Sydney closed her eyes and listened. She felt herself slowly drifting off to sleep.

Shep coughed, cleared his throat and said, "Just before you conk out there, Syd, it's my turn to ask you a couple of questions, if you don't mind," Shep said.

"I don't mind," Sydney said, starting awake. She suddenly remembered her plan to keep Shep talking all night so that Turk could sleep in his bed, so she sat straight up and forced her eyes wide open in an effort to stay alert.

"For starters, why are you two running away from home?"

"We're not really. We're actually looking for a home. We don't have a home to run away from," Sydney said.

That was at least half true, and Sydney hoped that Shep would be satisfied with her answer and not ask any more questions on the subject. She felt far too tired to make stuff up right then, even though she was generally pretty good at that sort of thing. Shep nodded with understanding, but then he continued.

"No mom or dad?" Shep asked.

"Our real mom died, and then our dad got another wife. She was really mean and she hated us and screamed at us all the time. Then one day she just kicked us out of the house for no good reason," Sydney explained.

"The evil stepmother, eh? It's the oldest story in the book," Shep said sympathetically.

That, too, was only half true. Their mother had died, but there was no evil stepmother to complain about. Instead, there was only their sad and lonely dad. But how could Sydney explain that to anyone? It was something even she couldn't understand. After their mother died, their dad became very sad. In fact, he became so sad that he stopped doing all the things a dad is supposed to do for his children. There was hardly ever proper food to eat or clean clothes to wear, birthdays went by without parties or cakes, and they started the school year without fresh school supplies or new shoes. There wasn't even a tree at Christmastime.

Not only did their dad stop looking after them, it seemed to Sydney that he could hardly even stand to look *at* them. Sydney came to believe that his sadness was because she and Turk reminded him too much of their mother—especially Sydney herself, who so resembled her mother in every way, including her red hair and bright green eyes, that people always felt the need to point it out. It wasn't long before Sydney decided that the best way they could help their dad to stop being so sad was if they weren't around anymore. She figured that if they weren't there to remind him of their mother, her dad would stop being sad and he could get better. Leaving him alone would be doing him the biggest favour she could think of. Or maybe Sydney was just plain mad at her dad. Maybe she just convinced herself that she was doing him a favour, when in fact what she was really trying to do by running away was to teach him a lesson. She'd show him that if he couldn't be bothered to take care of them, they could just as easily get by without him.

Whatever the truth of the matter was, Shep seemed to accept the story of the evil stepmother, which was yet another one of the little candy lies Sydney was so good at telling. He pondered it for a moment, then stood up, stretched, yawned, and scratched all around his long scraggly orange beard.

"Well! Time for bed. I need all the beauty rest I can get," Shep said, as he crushed the tiny camp fire with his blue cowboy boot.

This caught Sydney completely by surprise, and she was stunned by the realization that her plan to keep Shep up talking all night wasn't going to work. She tried to stand up too, but was so heavy with fatigue that she couldn't lift herself off the stump. She paused, gathered all of her strength, and then lurched wearily to her feet.

"Okay," Sydney said, dizzy from the effort of standing, "Just give me a second to wake up my little brother and we'll be on our way."

"On your way where? Face the facts, Syd—you've got no place to go," Shep said. "Tell you what, why don't you just leave your little brother right where he is? There's enough room in there for you, too. I've got another place to sleep, for emergency purposes only, in case of unexpected guests or if someone decides to burn my house down. I got a nest by the riverbank, made out of broken marriage mattresses. Suits me just fine. You and your brother can stay here for the night. In fact, you can stay here for as long as you want. And so, Sydney and her little brother whose name I do not yet know, good night, good night, and good night . . ."

As he said his good nights, Shep began walking slowly backwards, all the while facing Sydney, until he disappeared from sight. Sydney stood there listening to him talk and then whistle, soft and sweet, until the sound slowly faded away and all was quiet.

"Good night," Sydney whispered to no one.

You can probably imagine how relieved Sydney felt that she didn't have to wake up Turk and go search for some other place for them to stay. She shuddered with pleasure in anticipation of finally being able to lie down and fall asleep. Then she crawled into the little house, pulled the car door shut, and snuggled into bed beside Turk. She was asleep before she knew it.

CHAPTER FOUR

PLAN B

Have you ever woken up very early in the morning and not known where you are or how you got there? Sometimes that can happen when you're visiting out of town or staying at a friend's house, and you might experience several moments of confusion before you figure it all out and remember everything. That is exactly what Turk experienced when the first pink light of dawn nudged him awake inside Shep McParlain's little house. Only in Turk's case, he truly had no idea where he was or how he had gotten there, no matter how hard he concentrated. He sat up and took in his surroundings, trying to make sense of things. But it was all too strange to comprehend.

The first thing Turk noticed was that he was sleeping on a bed made out of car seats and cardboard, and the blankets on top of him were old winter coats and rags stitched together. All around on the walls and ceiling were pots and pans, parts from broken TVs and radios, pieces of mirror, shards of glass and broken plates, and dozens of pictures of animals torn from magazines—mostly monkeys, but also birds, horses, dogs and cats, and other animals as well, even a few dinosaurs. Looming over the foot of the bed was a huge framed painting of a group of dogs, all dressed in fancy clothes, sitting around a table playing cards and smoking cigars.

The weird chaos of the tiny room was alarming enough, but what was even worse was that the place was buzzing and bouncing with a million mosquitoes. They must have been feasting on Turk and Sydney all night, because both of them were covered in bites. Turk slapped one that was zipping in for another drink of blood from his neck.

At that moment, Turk would have believed that he and Sydney were staying in the home of some talking dogs in a junkyard on Mars. You could've told him that, and he'd have believed you. That's just how confused he was by waking up in Shep McParlain's little shack beside the Rat River.

There was only one thing for him to do.

"Sydney!" he shouted. "Quick! Wake up!"

Sydney didn't budge. She was deep asleep, all curled up and quietly snoring. A mosquito had just landed on her forehead, so Turk thought he'd do her the favour of slapping it before it added another bite bump to her already terribly bitten face.

"Ow!" Sydney cried.

"Sydney! Wake up! Where in the heck are we?" Turk demanded.

It took Sydney a moment to come to her senses and remember where they were.

"We're . . . well, I'm not—I think we're . . . oh yeah! We're at Shep McParlain's house," she said with relief, before rolling over and plunging back to sleep.

"Oh, good," Turk said. "That explains everything. Sydney! Would you please wake up! Who in the heck is Shep McWhatshisname and what are we doing in his house?"

Sydney sat up on her elbows and looked around blearily. The previous night in the dark and in her fatigue, the interior of the little house had appeared neat and tidy, even luxurious. The bed looked like a proper bed, the blankets looked like proper blankets, and none of the pictures and assorted other bizarre items hanging everywhere were even visible. But now, with the shafts of bright morning light piercing through the cracks in the walls and ceiling, Sydney's eyes were open to the oddities that Turk had been struggling to make sense of ever since he'd woken up.

"Holy moly," Sydney observed, "What a dump! And it's full of freaking mosquitoes! Wait! Oh my god. I think I've been bitten!" she yelped, swatting a mosquito away from her face.

"No kidding? I already know it's a dump that's full of mosquitoes," Turk said, trying to remain calm. "What I *don't* know is who Shep McWhatever his name is, and why we're staying in this house made out of garbage."

"C'mon!" Sydney said, crawling out of the bed and pushing open the car door. "Let's get out of here. I can explain everything."

As they walked along the trail and made their way toward the mall, Sydney told Turk all that had happened the previous night. Of course Turk was astonished to learn that they'd ended up sleeping in the house of that crazy bird man they'd seen behind the mall.

"He's not that crazy actually," Sydney said. "Well, I mean, of course he is sort of crazy. But it's the kind of crazy that makes sense, if you're forced to sit there and listen to him all night. Or at least *he* thinks he makes sense. So that means we're all crazy, when you think about it, because whatever you do makes sense to you, even if everyone else thinks you're crazy. You know what I mean?"

"No," Turk said. "I don't. I think you went crazy too, just from talking with that crazy bird man all night."

"Hey, that reminds me. I owe him one Hawaiian doughnut," Sydney said.

"See? You've gone completely mental."

It was still very early in the morning, and the only place open was the Chubby Princess Doughnut Cottage situated in the parking lot between the mall and the gas bar. Turk and Sydney entered and walked up to the counter. The heavenly smell of fresh baked goods greeted them, and they gazed with longing at the stunning assortment of doughnuts in the display case—five hundred varieties in all—while waiting to be served. It wasn't until the man working behind the counter turned to face them from filling the coffee machine that they recognized him. It was Kumar, wearing a tan brown doughnut shop uniform with bright gold trim.

"Good morning!" Kumar beamed merrily. "How might I help. . . ." The sunny smile vanished from his face.

". . . you? Well then. What have we here? If it isn't Sydney and her small brother Turk! We finally meet again," Kumar said sternly.

"But . . . Kumar. What are you doing here? Do you? Wait a minute. Don't you work at the gas bar?" Sydney stammered.

"Yes, of course," Kumar replied. "I am currently working at many, many jobs. Right around the clock I am working. It's for my children back in India, you see. But enough about me already. Have you brought your father? I was waiting to discuss matters with him yesterday most eagerly, as promised. And yet he did not come. Why, may I ask?"

Turk looked at Sydney, expecting to hear one of those little candy lies that she was so quick to produce. But Sydney only stood there with her mouth hanging open, too caught out to know what to say.

Turk decided that it was his turn to give it a try.

"Our father works as a spy for the government," Turk began earnestly. "He got called away for a secret spy mission and didn't come home until very late last night, so we didn't get a chance to talk to him before bedtime."

"Really?" said Kumar, in obvious disbelief.

"Yeah. Really," Turk continued, not knowing how to stop. "And then this morning our dog ran away. So our dad went to look for him. He borrowed a helicopter from the government to go searching for the dog. But then … uhm … the helicopter ran out of gas, so he phoned us from Mexico on our top secret satellite phone and told us to come here and get breakfast."

"Incredible," Kumar said. "And all of this is true?" he asked sharply, looking at Sydney.

"Ah. Yeah. Well, sort of," Sydney said, with a tiny fake laugh. "Except the part about the government spy. And also the thing about the helicopter, and running out of gas. That's not quite true. And Mexico. But the dog really did run away. And so I guess everything else is true," she said, with a forced smile.

"I am completely flabbergasted," Kumar said. "Now, more than ever, I would like to meet with your father. Just to sort out all of this confusion in my mind. The next time I see you, please promise me, it will be with your father."

A big-bellied tow truck driver had pushed up behind Turk and Sydney. "Hey, buddy. Hurry it up there, would ya?" he demanded rudely.

"Yes, sir," Kumar smiled. "So. What would you be wanting for your breakfast?"

Sydney, embarrassed and desperate to escape, quickly but politely asked for three bagels with cream cheese, three bottles of apple juice, and three Hawaiian doughnuts.

"Why three of everything?" Kumar wanted to know.

Turk jumped right in, "Well, because for our dad. For when he gets back from Mexico."

Sydney could only roll her eyes.

When they got back outside and were walking across the parking lot with their food, Sydney stopped and faced her little brother. "Listen, Turk," she said, "the thing about little candy lies is that they have to be little. Like this." She held her thumb and finger a teensy bit apart. "You told one that was like this," Sydney said, spreading her arms out wide. "That doesn't work. When it's that big, people want to have a real good look at it. Keep it small and sweet and they don't even notice. What you told was a big fat stinking fish lie. That, they notice."

Turk was disappointed to hear this. He thought his first attempt at telling a little candy lie had gone rather well. He especially liked the part about the helicopter searching for their missing dog in Mexico. Who wouldn't want to believe that?

"Anyways," Sydney continued, "don't worry about it. I've got something really great to tell you. It's our Plan B. I'll tell you all about it while we're eating. You're going to love it. I can't wait to see the look on your face when you hear it. Let's go!"

***

Sydney took off running toward the river and Turk ran along after her. They ran behind the mall and found the river trail. When they got back to the clearing, there was

Shep, whistling away and hard at work making improvements to his house. He had found a broken toy piano that he figured would make a fine addition to his roof.

"Amazing what people throw out, isn't it?" he asked somewhat sadly as Sydney and Turk emerged from the trees. "A perfectly excellent musical instrument just left in the trash. Oh well—their loss is my pain."

After carefully fitting the toy piano into place on the roof, Shep tilted his head to listen as he tapped on one of the keys. It produced a dull little *blang* sound that was as soft as a whisper. "See? A fine and serviceable doorbell."

Turk stayed on the edge of the clearing, behind Sydney and well away from the shack. He was watching Shep warily, and wondering why exactly they'd come back here and how soon they could leave. Sydney glanced back over her shoulder at Turk and waved at him to step forward. Turk stayed right where he was.

"Shep? I'd like you to meet my brother Turk. Turk, this is Shep McParlain Jr.," Sydney said.

"Turk, eh? Interesting name," Shep said. "Might you hail from Constantinople, perhaps?"

"No, no," Sydney said. "We hail from Parkdale. His name's actually Curtis. Curt for short. When he was little, he used to put his clothes on backwards all the time, so we called him Turk, cause it's like Curt, only sort of spelled backwards."

"I'm very glad to meet you, Turk. Or should I call you Sitruc? And please accept my most sincere apologies for not being here to greet you this morning. Not very polite of me as your host, I must admit. *Mea culpa*. My alarm didn't go off for some reason," Shep said, examining and shaking the giant alarm clock attached to the bicycle chain around his neck.

Turk silently thanked his lucky stars that Shep's clock had failed him. It had been bad enough to wake up inside that crazy little shack, but to be greeted by Shep McParlain first thing in the morning would have given Turk a shock from which he might have never fully recovered.

"That's okay," Turk said meekly.

"Let's eat," Sydney said cheerfully, "I'm starving!"

They all sat around a miniature toy pool table that Shep told them he used only for special occasions or very important people. He was delighted with the apple juice and the bagels and cream cheese, but especially with the Hawaiian doughnut, which he said was his very favourite kind. The only time he ever got to eat any though, was when they made too many at the doughnut shop and had to throw some out. He carefully picked each individual candy sprinkle off his doughnut and savoured them one at a time, while explaining that he got all his food out of the garbage, mostly from the dumpsters behind The Big Giant People Food Store at the mall.

"I've got some pork chops for dinner tonight if you like, barely used and almost new," he said. "And some extra large cabbages I've been saving up for weeks. Grade B export quality."

Turk didn't find this to be very appetizing table talk, but at least he was starting to feel a little more at ease around

Shep, mostly because Sydney was so relaxed and pleasant with him.

"Thanks Shep," Sydney said. "But I think we'll eat at home tonight for a change."

"At home? Wait a minute there, Syd. Last night you had me believing you had no home. By the way, the pink ones are simply sensational at this time of year," Shep said as he delicately nibbled on a single pink candy sprinkle off his doughnut.

Sydney's green eyes gleamed with excitement. This big idea, which had come to her the night before when she was all alone and there was no one around to share it with, had just kept growing bigger and more fantastically perfect in her mind. By now she was truly desperate to talk about it.

"We don't have a home—yet," Sydney said, springing to her feet. What she had to say was way too important to be explained while sitting down. "But we're going to go shopping for one today. Right now. In The Royal Woods!"

"Better bring a big bag of money, Syd," Shep said. "Those new houses must cost an oodle or two of dough."

"On no, see, we're not going to actually buy one," Sydney said, pacing about excitedly as she pitched her idea. "We're just going to *borrow* one. It's like the houses are for free in there. Have you seen how many of them are just sitting empty? I'd say, like, about half of them are. We'll shop around till we find one we like, on a nice street with friendly neighbours. And then we'll just move right in, and pretend like it's ours. Who'll know it isn't? And if someone comes along and buys the house we're in, we'll just move to another one. Isn't that the greatest idea ever, Turk?"

Actually, Turk didn't think it was the greatest idea ever, but he couldn't say exactly why he thought that, so he didn't say anything. What he feared was that this was another one of those so-called great ideas they'd both been having lately, the ones that turned out to be not so great after all. Like riding on the outside of a train, or getting cleaned up in a car wash, or sleeping in a house made out of garbage that turned out to be packed full of mosquitoes.

Turk sat thinking about Sydney's great idea, hoping that Shep might give them some sound reasons why her plan was bad and certain to fail. After all, Turk thought, Shep appeared to be an experienced man of the world, and probably had a good deal of first-hand knowledge about bad ideas. Turk looked hopefully at Shep, who was scratching his orange beard while gravely contemplating Sydney's proposal.

Finally, Shep announced his conclusion. "That is a great idea, Syd. You are quite clearly a living genius. I'd have probably come up with that idea myself," he mused, "but you see, I've always preferred to live in custom-built homes. All those new houses look exactly the same to me, and they all got that new house smell and the look-at-me Type A personality. I'd find that a bit cold and alienating myself. But for you two youngsters, you might not experience it that way. Yep. You are one sharp cookie, Syd, no doubt about it."

Shep nodded his head in admiration while Sydney beamed with pride. Turk was the only one who wasn't enjoying the moment. What he found especially frustrating was that he couldn't say exactly *why* he thought it to be such a bad idea. He just had a feeling. But then he thought of something.

"Wouldn't that be sort of like stealing?" he asked.

"How do you mean?" Sydney said.

"Well, I mean, like, we don't own the house. We'll just be living there like we do own it. But someone else *does* own it, and so it's like we're stealing it from them."

"But they're not using it, so why should they even care?" Sydney pointed out. "What about this, Turk—where is your bike right now?"

"Rodney has it."

"Why?"

"Because he's my best friend and I wasn't going to use it this summer, so I gave it to him."

"Exactly. You weren't going to use it so you gave it to Rodney to use. That's just like what we're going to do. It's just like Rodney using your bike."

"No, it isn't." Turk argued, "I told Rodney he could use my bike. No one told us we could use their house."

Shep was following this conversation with intense interest, looking from one to the other and nodding in agreement with whoever was speaking at the time. "Very impressive debate," he said. "As a former philosopher myself, I must say that you both make excellent use of logic and ethics in your respective argumentations."

Sydney chose to ignore Shep and stay focused on her little brother. She was intent on convincing Turk of the brilliance of her idea, and was disappointed that he hadn't recognized it instantly.

"Look, those houses are where the farm is supposed to be. And who owned that farm? Our relatives did, that's who! So it's almost like it was our farm. And what happened to our farm? Those houses came and chased it away, that's what. So why can't we borrow one of the houses for a while? It's not like we're going to take it anywhere. We'll leave it right where we found it when we're done. We won't break anything or take anything."

Shep watched Turk eagerly, expecting him to come up with an equally powerful and convincing point. But Turk only stared at his own feet, not knowing what to say.

"Besides which," Sydney said very gently, "we've got no choice. We've got no place else to go now."

Turk would have liked to say, "What about going home?" But he knew that they had done their secret handshake promise—two snaps, two slaps, and one long palm slide—to not do that or even to mention it out loud. And Turk was always true to his word.

"Birds sometimes use the nests of other birds when they find them empty," Shep reflected quietly. "Bears move into the caves of other bears when the cold of winter arrives. A jackfish doesn't tell all the other jackfish that he owns one special hole in the lake, and no one else can come there to swim when he's not around. The magnificent migrating mallard stops for the night in any farm pond or swamp whichsoever he desires. The duck-billed platypus is known to—"

"Okay, okay," Turk interrupted. "I get it already." He sighed, stood up and forced himself to smile for Sydney's sake. "Let's go house shopping. But after that, we've got to for sure start looking for Uncle Frank and Aunt Lily."

"You're the best, Turk," Sydney said. "We'll leave our stuff here and just go have a look. Is that okay, Shep?"

But Shep was lost in thought. "The flying squirrel has no words or concept of permanent abode, let alone Private Property or No Trespassing," he continued, staring into the distance.

Sydney and Turk slipped away, leaving Shep there lecturing himself as the bright morning sun climbed up over the trees and warmed the little clearing beside the Rat River.

CHAPTER FIVE

A HOME WITH A VIEW

S hep was certainly right about one thing—all of the houses in The Royal Woods did look pretty much the same. Wherever Sydney and Turk found themselves in the maze of brand new streets and bays and cul-de-sacs, they kept thinking that they'd been there before and were just walking around in circles. Every house had a huge garage in front, a treeless yard of black dirt all around, and a picture window that stared straight across the street at the same house staring right back. Only about half of the houses had curtains in the windows, or a car or boat in the drive-way, suggesting that people might actually live inside. As they wandered around, Sydney and Turk tried to sort out where they were and where they'd been by memorizing the names of the streets. But that wasn't very helpful since all the names had something to do with royalty, making them easy to confuse. It was hard to remember if they'd already been on Prince Lane or Queen Bay, when minutes later they'd find themselves on Princess Path or King Way. It wasn't long before they were completely lost.

What made it all especially eerie is that The Royal Woods was so big and open and quiet. Sydney and Turk were used to living in a city, filled with noise and people and things happening everywhere. But there was no one and nothing to be seen in The Royal Woods. Except for every once in a while when someone in a car would glide by and stare at them, as though it were something amazing to see two human beings outside walking. Sydney would stick her tongue out at them, and the people in the car would quickly look away.

"We'll really have to get a car to fit in around here," Sydney said.

"Yeah," Turk keenly agreed. "And let's get cable TV, too."

"Let's find a house first."

All this trudging about on the empty streets and past the identical houses of The Royal Woods put Sydney in a sour mood. She had started out on their quest full of optimism. This had promised to be a fun adventure, and she'd thought The Royal Woods would be a fresh and exciting place to explore. But her enthusiasm faded as the day got hotter and everything began to take on a strange and lonely cast. The sprawling emptiness of the place made her feel small and unwanted. The Royal Woods was so new and clean and quiet, and the only living thing there seemed to be the wind. It was hard for her to believe that this had all once been Uncle Frank and Aunt Lily's cluttered and lively farm. There wasn't the smallest hint that a farm had ever even existed there. It was even harder for her to believe that she could ever be happy living in this strange new place.

In a brooding funk, Sydney led Turk up one street and down another, around bays and in and out of cul-de-sacs, not even looking at the houses anymore, and not uttering a single word.

Even though Sydney had been careful not to mention anything about the farm, Turk knew what she was thinking. That's what inspired him to come up with a pretty good idea.

"Instead of thinking about what the houses look *like*," he suggested, "let's think about what the houses look *at*."

"How do you mean?" Sydney grumbled.

"I mean, let's pick a house with a farm view. They're all the same anyways, so let's find one that reminds us about the farm."

Sydney wasn't sure about the idea, but she was content to let Turk take the lead for a change. With renewed purpose, they headed south to the very edge of The Royal Woods, where they came to a street called Court Jester Way. At the first house they found, they marched up the driveway, turned their backs to the garage, and looked out. There was nothing to see but the big flat prairie and the even bigger blue sky, all the way to North Dakota.

"Sold," Sydney said, smiling with relief and delight. "You're brilliant, Turk. It's just like we're back on the old farm."

Sydney yanked the *For Sale* sign out of the ground at the bottom of the driveway and dropped it in the black dirt. It was the same sign that sat out front of every vacant house in The Royal Woods. It featured a picture of two smiling, sun tanned chubby faces over the words, "Call Bob and Barb Buick—your exclusive Realtors in The Royal Woods."

"Thanks for everything, Bob and Barb," Sydney said. "We'll take over from here."

Now all they had to do was discover what their new house looked like on the inside. That's when they hit an obstacle they probably should have anticipated in the first place. The doors were all locked. First they tried the front door. Then they walked around to the back of the house on some boards put down on the mud as a temporary sidewalk. But the back door was locked too. And so was the garage.

"How in the heck are we supposed to get in?" Sydney wondered. "We don't want to break anything. Do we?"

"No," Turk said emphatically. "We certainly do *not* want to break anything."

"It sure does look nice in there though, eh?" Sydney said, pressing her face to the window at the back of the house. "Oh, my my. A sunny kitchen nook, split-level dining and entertainment area. And look! A lovely fireplace. At least three well-appointed bathrooms, I bet. And best of all, not a single mosquito or car part in sight."

"Remember your promise, Sydney. You said we wouldn't break anything or take anything," Turk reminded her.

Turk knew that Sydney was capable of doing almost anything once she set her mind on a course of action. But he wasn't going to allow her to do anything bad, no matter what she said. Sydney was in a dangerous mood though, and Turk watched her uneasily. All that morning she had gotten more and more angry about the farm disappearing, and frustrated by The Royal Woods that had taken its place. So now that they had finally found a house she could actually imagine living in, she wanted to occupy the place immediately. She felt entitled to do whatever she wanted in The Royal Woods, as though the very streets and houses owed her something for having replaced the beloved farm. Sydney walked all around the house, trying every window and exploring every possible way in. But it was locked up tight as a drum.

"If we could get you up on the roof, probably you could slip down the chimney," she said squinting up at the top of the two story house.

"Slip? Or do you mean fall? I don't believe in Santa Clause anymore, for your information. And what if I get stuck?" Turk said.

"Good point," Sydney agreed.

Turk felt increasingly nervous watching Sydney. She looked like a big prowling red cat trying to bust into its own house for dinner. He feared that any second she would find a rock and "accidentally" smash a window. The tension was becoming unbearable.

"Let's just go back to Shep's place," Turk urged.

"Yeah, good idea. Maybe we can help him cook up those used pork chops and the extra large cabbages for dinner," Sydney said, tugging at a basement window.

"No, not to eat dinner. I'm not sure, but maybe he'll have some ideas about what we can do. He seems to know about a lot of things. Let's just try him."

"Well, we need to get our backpacks anyway," Sydney said. "But I'm for sure not sleeping at his place again. I'm still not finished scratching all the bites I got last night."

Sydney didn't have much hope that Shep could actually help them, but she thought that maybe she'd get the chance to leave Turk at Shep's place for a bit, and then she'd sneak back by herself to find some way into the house. Any way into the house.

<hr />

It was dusk when they got back to the shack by the river. They got there to find Shep loading his shopping cart with supplies and furnishings for their new house. A lot of the things were actually quite useful, including a couple of slightly used sleeping bags, some pots and pans, knives and forks, and a set of cracked up dollhouse plates and cups. But a lot of it was also completely useless, like the part from a broken washing machine, a half bag of kitty litter, a single red plaid house slipper, and some soggy Halloween decorations.

"That's all great stuff, Shep," Sydney said. "But I'm afraid we don't have a house to put it in. The house we want is all locked up, and we certainly don't want to break anything to get in, do we?"

"We don't?" Shep asked.

"No, we don't," Turk insisted. "We already decided about that."

"Well that's no problem," Shep said. "There's more than one way to peel a banana. Give me a second here and I'll change into my construction clothes. We'll just see about that so-called locked house."

Turk wasn't very keen on having Shep actually come with them to help solve their predicament. He'd vaguely hoped that Shep would magically provide them with some great new idea for where they could live, and then they could be on their way. Turk was even less keen on having Shep accompany them when he saw him emerge from his shack wearing his "construction clothes." He still wore his canary yellow tuxedo jacket, one blue cowboy boot and one red running shoe (although for some reason he was now wearing them on the opposite feet), the alarm clock tied to the bicycle chain around his neck, and the white satin gloves. But in addition to all that, he now had on a big pair of orange and terribly grease-stained mechanic's coveralls under his jacket, and a sky-blue construction hard hat on his head.

"Let's get to work," he said, striding robustly through the clearing. "First stop, hardware store. Bring cash money."

Turk and Sydney grabbed their backpacks and had to sprint to keep up with Shep. His loping lopsided gate was faster than a normal person's flat out running speed. Wearing a running shoe with a cowboy boot only seemed to give Shep additional quickness. Down the trail and then out into the mall parking lot they flew, dodging cars and dashing after Shep across the open pavement. They arrived at the doors to the Jack-in-a-Big-Box Hardware Emporium, where Shep came to a sudden halt. He became quite serious and solemn, as though they were entering a cathedral.

"After you," Shep said gravely, and in they went.

The place was as vast and sprawling as an airport terminal. There was row after row of towering shelves, stocked with every imaginable tool, building supply, and home decor item. Turk followed along behind Shep and Sydney, who were intensely discussing the many thousands of products on the shelves. New things had a special significance for Shep, since he only ever used things that people had already owned and thrown away. Seeing all these new items was, for Shep, like a scientist discovering the very beginnings of life.

"Excuse me, my good man," Shep said to a clerk who was bent over stocking shelves with remote-controlled wildlife lawn ornaments. "Where might we find your tiniest available screwdriver?"

And so, for the second time that day, Sydney and Turk had a surprise encounter with Kumar. Wearing a candy-striped hardware store clerk uniform, Kumar turned away from his shelving work to face them.

"Kumar?" Sydney and Turk said, at exactly the same time, with exactly the same surprise in their voices. But Kumar himself was experiencing an even bigger surprise.

"Sydney? Turk? And could it be? This is your father?" Kumar asked, looking with astonishment at Shep.

Shep was amused to hear him say this, and was just about to answer when Sydney blurted out, "Yes. Yes, it is. Um . . . Kumar? This is Dad. Dad, this is Kumar."

The two men shook hands uncertainly—Shep because he couldn't understand why he was supposed to be pretending that he was their dad, and Kumar because, well, for a number of reasons, including the fact that he'd never in his life shaken hands with a man wearing ladies' satin gloves before. But more so because he had seen Shep many times, digging food and things out of the dumpsters behind the mall, and whistling away as he pushed his shopping cart full of trash across the parking lot. Kumar decided that there wasn't much point in asking such a man why he allowed his children to use the car wash to shower, and he also now understood why Turk had told such extravagant lies about his father. Still, Kumar felt a duty to question this man a little, mostly out of concern for the well-being of the two young children, Sydney and Turk, for whom he had begun to feel fondly protective.

"I believe, sir, that I have seen you on occasion," Kumar began cautiously, "in and around and behind the mall. In the garbage area. Looking for . . . things. Would it be impudent of me to ask why you leave your children to fend for themselves while pursuing such activities?"

"Well, um . . . good question Mr. Kumar. And very well put," Shep said, trying to think of a reasonable explanation to account for himself. His eyes widened with satisfaction when he thought of exactly what to say.

"So you see, the thing is, please don't tell anyone, sir, but I am a secret government spy on a top secret mission investigating, basically, shopping mall dumpsters. And you know how it is. Sometimes you just have to put your work ahead of the family."

Shep smiled and patted the heads of his two children.

Kumar tried to smile back, but his face twisted in bewilderment. "A secret government spy?" he asked weakly.

Turk nodded seriously, and Sydney had to look away, trying not to laugh. Kumar assumed that this must be the story that the man told his children in order to account for his eccentric lifestyle. Either that, or it was all true and he really was in fact a secret government spy. Meaning that Kumar was now living in the weirdest place on the entire planet.

"And now, if you would be so kind, could you please direct us to the miniature screwdriver section?" Shep asked.

"Certainly, sir. Aisle 75. And by the way. Have you found your dog?"

"Our dog?" Shep asked. "Ah, yes, the dog. We did find the dog. He phoned us from Acapulco this morning. Thanks for asking."

As Kumar stood watching the unlikely trio walk away, he resolved to keep an eye out for Sydney and Turk. They were clearly in need of whatever assistance he could provide.

On the long walk to aisle 75, they had a lot of time to talk about what had happened with Kumar. Shep wasn't at all bothered that they'd lied about him being their father. In fact, he rather liked the idea of assuming that role.

"You two really do need a responsible adult in your life," he said. "And since there aren't any of those presently available, you might as well use me for the job."

Turk, on the other hand, was beginning to feel terribly uncomfortable with all the gigantic fibs they'd been telling Kumar. He seemed like a really nice guy. Why should they keep lying to him?

"You're right, Turk," Sydney agreed, reading his thoughts. "Kumar is a really nice guy. I just don't know if we can tell him the truth right now. If he knew the real story about us, maybe he'd get all upset and even call the cops or something. We'll wait and see. One thing's for sure, we'll definitely be running into him again. He must work in every single place in The Royal Woods. When does the poor guy get a chance to sleep?"

By then Shep's attention had drifted away from Turk and Sydney's discussion, and he was lost in a pleasant daydream. He strolled along with a big smile on his face, whistling merrily and enjoying his newfound fatherhood role.

"Come along then, children," he said, beaming with parental pride, "aisle 75 is right this way."

There were well over one thousand screwdrivers to choose from in aisle 75. After a few minutes of searching and whistling, Shep found the tiniest screwdriver ever made. It was no bigger than a toothpick.

Then they set off for Court Jester Way, back to the house that Sydney and Turk had found earlier that day. Much to Turk's relief, they didn't encounter a single person as they passed through The Royal Woods. Even though he'd gotten used to being around Shep, and actually liked him quite a lot, Turk was somewhat of a shy boy who didn't like attracting attention to himself. Try as he might, he couldn't quite get over his embarrassment at the odd looks they got from the people who saw them. As for Sydney, she never concerned herself with such things, and rather enjoyed walking around in public with Shep, just to see how people reacted. Especially at the mall.

When they got to the house, it only took Shep a couple of seconds to open the back door lock with the tiny screwdriver.

"Three years of locksmith school finally pays off," he said proudly.

Sydney was the first into the house, followed by Turk and then Shep, who stood hesitantly just inside the door way. "Just as I suspected. It's got that new-house smell I was worried about," Shep said, sniffing the air.

He was right. The house smelled completely new. It was the smell of fresh white paint and newly cut and hammered wood and drywall. Everything about the house felt new and untouched; even the echoing sound of their own voices and footsteps seemed somehow brand new. Sydney and Turk rambled freely all over the place, exploring every room, closet, cupboard and drawer. It had everything they needed, including a stove and fridge, a washer and dryer, and three well-appointed bathrooms, just as Sydney had predicted. Best of all, they'd both have their own bedrooms on the second floor, each with a nice view of the prairie out front. Sydney was elated and Turk was pretty much convinced that this was, after all, a great idea. The greatest idea ever, in fact. He'd never even been in such a big sparkling clean new house before, let alone lived in one. Shep was the only one who seemed uneasy.

"It's great! Everything about it is perfect. Come on in, Shep. Have a look around," Sydney urged. But Shep stayed hovering just inside the back door, looking awkward and anxious to leave.

"No. No thanks, don't think I will. I haven't been inside a regular house since April the first, 1977, and this one's a bit too rich and filling for me to start back in with. I'd have to build myself up slowly for a house like this. Maybe I could begin by visiting the garage for a couple of weeks, just to get used to the idea. Meanwhile, I'll be out in the backyard, enjoying the wind," he said, as he walked backwards out the door.

Sydney and Turk were disappointed by Shep's response to their new house. They went out back to try to talk him into coming inside, but he refused. Finally it was agreed that instead of Shep visiting them at their house, Sydney and Turk would go everyday for a visit to Shep's place. He was happy with that idea. "After all," he said, "I am your official father now. It was publicly proclaimed at the mall."

They went back to Shep's place to fetch the supplies that he'd gathered for them. Shep insisted that he push the shopping cart over to the new house, saying that they were both too young to drive. After they got everything in order and were all nicely moved in, Shep suggested that they celebrate with a sumptuous pork chop and cabbage banquet at his place.

"Not tonight," Sydney said. "Tonight it's our treat. You've done so much to help us, Shep. We can never thank you enough. Tonight we'll take you to eat anyplace you like."

They all enjoyed a big meal at the Tijuana Speedy Burrito in the mall, and then they walked Shep back to his place before returning to the house on Court Jester Way. Sydney and Turk were both completely exhausted by then, and anxious to see what it was like to sleep in comfortable sleeping bags in their nice new bedrooms for the first time. Everything turned out to be perfect, and they slept wonderfully well and woke up late the next morning feeling refreshed and happy.

Here is where you might be thinking this story should end—with Sydney and Turk living happily ever after in their big new house in The Royal Woods. You could stop reading here if you want, and leave Sydney and Turk right where they are, imagining to yourself that all their troubles are over and that they finally had everything they needed. To make it yet more perfect, you can even picture them running into Uncle Frank and Aunt Lily, just by chance at the mall. And then they could live happily ever after together in their big new house. Wouldn't that be sweet?

However, if you do decide to read on, you'll soon see that this isn't the way things went at all, and that their story was far from done.

For one thing, when Sydney dug into the side pocket of her backpack to get some money to buy breakfast the next morning, she discovered that all they had left was six dollars and thirty-seven cents.

CHAPTER SIX

HEAVEN'S GOLF BALLS

As you are no doubt well aware, six dollars and thirty-seven cents is not very much money. It might be enough money to take a couple of your friends out for ice cream sundaes, or to rent a movie and buy some popcorn for a sleepover at your cousin's place. But it's certainly not enough money for a twelve-year-old girl and her eight-year-old brother to start a new life in a modern suburban subdivision. In fact, it turned out to be just exactly enough money to buy the identical breakfast Sydney and Turk had bought the previous day at the Chubby Princess Doughnut Cottage.

Kumar was working there again that morning, and when he noticed the cautious way that Sydney counted out and handed over the last of their money, he realized instantly that the two children were in serious financial difficulty. He was far too discreet to ask them about the matter directly. Instead, without them seeing it, he slipped three extra bagels with cream cheese and as many doughnuts into their takeout bag.

"If you wish, come by later to the gas bar when I am working this evening. I would like to treat you to some tasty samosas," Kumar smiled. "And bring your father too, won't you?"

"Gee thanks, Kumar. You're the best," Sydney said, not exactly certain what samosas were, but sincerely touched by his generosity. Turk mumbled thanks as well, with his eyes glued to the floor. He felt so ashamed by all their fibbing to this kind and considerate man that he couldn't even look Kumar in the face anymore.

"Holy moly," Sydney said looking into the bag as they journeyed across the parking lot. "Kumar threw in some free bagels! And extra doughnuts, too!"

That news only made Turk feel worse. For Sydney, however, it was a sure sign that things were going to be okay. They had overcome every difficulty they'd encountered so far on their adventure, and today they faced yet another formidable challenge. She couldn't help but feel optimistic about their prospects, given that they'd barely started out on this bright sunny morning, and already they'd had their first bit of good luck.

Shep was nowhere to found when they arrived at the clearing beside the Rat River. Turk rang the toy piano doorbell on the house, while Sydney called out for him down by the river. But there was no answer, and no sound of whistling, except for the twittering of the birds in the trees. The place felt weirdly quiet and empty without Shep bustling about, chattering to himself and whistling away. After looking around a bit more, they sat down at the miniature pool table to eat breakfast and discuss their plans for the day, both eagerly anticipating Shep's arrival any second. It was amazing to think that they'd only known Shep for less than a day and a half. In that short time, he had become a vital person in their lives.

"We've got to make some money, Turk. Any bright ideas?" Sydney asked, sipping her apple juice from a straw.

"Hey, I know! Maybe Kumar could give you one of his jobs. He's got at least three of them. Probably he'd let you borrow one," Turk said.

"I can't get a proper job with a uniform and everything. I'm not old enough, so they won't let me. We have to figure out some other kind of work that isn't really a job but that makes tons of money anyway."

Turk thought about that while starting in on his Hawaiian doughnut. Eating that doughnut naturally brought his mind around to Shep. "When Shep gets here, I'll bet he'll have some ideas about what we can do. He's full of them," he said.

"I wouldn't be so sure about that. Don't get me wrong—Shep knows about a lot of things—but I don't think he knows much about money, judging by his lifestyle. He doesn't even use money. I bet he's not interested in the subject."

Those words were barely out of Sydney's mouth when something went whizzing across the pool table and struck Shep's house with a loud bang. Sydney and Turk jumped up. Then something else flew into the clearing and bounced off a tree. Golf balls! Someone was firing golf balls at them. They looked all around, trying to figure out where they were coming from, when a voice from beyond the trees called, "There he is! Fire!" Another golf ball slammed into the house.

"Hey!" Sydney yelled, "What do you think you're doing?!"

Three boys peeked out from their hiding places above the clearing. "Hold your fire men," one of them barked, his voice full of importance. "It's just some little kids."

A skinny boy, about the same age as Sydney, with a pointy nose and chin and small hard dark eyes, swaggered into the clearing. The slogan on his T-shirt said "YOU STINK." The other two boys marched up behind him. All three of them wore camouflaged pants, baseball hats on backwards, and big new gleaming white running shoes. The boy with the pointy face seemed to be the leader of the other two, who were chubby identical twins, one shouldering a gigantic Super Soaker water gun.

"Who are you calling a little kid, kid?" Sydney fumed. "And what's with throwing golf balls at us?"

"Where'd he go?" the pointy faced boy demanded.

"Where did who go?" Sydney responded angrily.

"That big dirty trash bird man, that's who. We've been chasing him all morning. But it looks like he escaped."

"He's not a big dirty trash bird man!" Sydney said, glaring furiously at the boy. "And what are you chasing him for? Why don't you just leave him alone?"

"Because we want to, that's why. And it's none of your business what we do, carrot head," the boy sneered.

Sydney could have jumped on that boy right then and there and taught him a very serious lesson. She was already burning mad about the golf balls, madder still when she discovered that they'd been chasing Shep around all morning. And then to be called a name by this disgusting little creature. Well, it was all together too much to take.

"Easy Sydney," Turk said quietly, his voice shaking.

"Listen here you little rat face, you'd better just turn around and go straight home if you know what's good for you," Sydney said levelly, her fists clenched like rocks.

If that boy took even one step in her direction, Turk knew that Sydney wouldn't be able to control herself, and that she'd fly at him with all her strength. The boy must have also realized how perilous the situation was, and decided that he had no desire to be beaten up by a girl in front of his friends. He grinned sourly, shrugged his shoulders and backed off a little. Sydney faked a quick move in his direction, and the boy flinched and backed off a little more.

"At ease men," he said to the twins, who were watching the proceedings with wide eyes and twitching nerves. "We'll make another recognizance sweep along the riverbank. If we can't establish his location, we'll circle back here to search and destroy the shack."

It was Turk's turn to get upset. "Why in the heck would you want to do that? It's his house, for Pete's sake. It's where he lives."

"It's not a house. It's just a pile of garbage," the boy said. "Everyone in The Royal Woods wants it, and him, out of here."

"But why?" Turk asked, completely bewildered.

"Because they're mean and stupid," Sydney said, "that's why. But don't worry, Turk. They're not going to do anything to Shep's house. You know why? Because I know where that little rodent boy lives. Whatever he does to Shep's house, I'm going do to his house."

"How do you know where I live?" the boy sneered.

"'Cause I'm a witch. I know everything," Sydney said, menacingly.

That gave the boy something to think about. Finding this wild red-haired girl on the riverbank, eating her take-out breakfast at a busted toy pool table beside the bird man's crazy shack, it was possible to believe that she really was a witch. He didn't know exactly what to make of this girl, but he sensed that she wasn't someone you'd want to overly provoke, witch or not. He stood there glowering at her, but all he could think of to say was, "Oh yeah?" To which Sydney of course replied, "Yeah."

Sydney and the boy locked threatening eyes for several silent moments, before one of the twins broke the tension. "You guys wouldn't happen to have any doughnuts left, would you?" he asked meekly. And the other twin added, "Are those Hawaiians? Mmmmm."

"Shut up, Chad. You too, Brad," the first boy muttered.

"See?" Sydney said to Turk. "He's even mean to his own friends. Go ahead. Have a doughnut, boys. Help yourselves."

The twins hesitated, glancing at one another, waiting to see who would make the first move. But not even the icy stare of their leader, nor the possibility that this wild girl might suddenly jump them, could overcome their craving for doughnuts. Together they cautiously approached the pool table, ready to bolt like bunnies at the first hint of danger. Turk handed each of them a doughnut from the bag.

"You want one?" Turk asked the other boy.

"Men! I order you not to eat those doughnuts. This could be a booby trap," the boy commanded.

"It doesn't taste like a booby trap," Chad said, chewing his doughnut thoughtfully.

"I love Hawaiians," Brad said, "You guys got anything to drink? I've been running around like a maniac all morning. I am truly dying of thirst. I already drank all the water from my Super Soaker."

"Oh my god," the first boy said in disgust, "I give up."

"Good idea," Sydney said. "Give up and go home. And I better not ever catch you around here again. Or else."

The boy sneered at her, just to make like he wasn't afraid and that he wasn't going to be bossed around by a girl.

"We're going to keep the golf balls," Sydney added. "Since you practically killed us with them. It's payment for the doughnuts."

"Fair enough," said Brad.

"Good deal," said Chad.

"Now go away," Sydney said. "My brother and I have more important things to do than play soldiers with a bunch of little kids."

"Yeah right," the boy said sarcastically, and then abruptly turned and marched back toward the trees, with Brad and Chad licking their fingers and scrambling to catch up with him.

"Wait a second! What's the other guy's name? The leader boy?" Sydney called out.

"Don't tell her my . . ." the boy yelled, but it was too late.

"Morton!" Brad called back over his shoulder.

". . . name," Morton finished with a groan. He spun around and screamed at Brad, "That's classified information! Loser!"

Glancing back at Sydney, Morton summoned up his most lethal death stare. "I'll be back," he muttered, like some guy in an action movie. Then he turned and stormed off. "Let's move out, men. Double quick time! Hey ya! Hup, two, three, four, hup, two, three, four . . ."

Sydney and Turk stood listening to the three boys march away. For a moment, they were stunned speechless in the wake of this unpleasant and disturbing encounter. All at once a welcome quiet fell over the clearing. Then Turk turned to his sister and asked in a whisper, "Morton?"

They both burst into helpless laughter. They howled, they roared, they yelped, they choked and they sputtered, and they hadn't quite contained their laughing when Sydney blurted out, "And don't forget Brad 'n' Chad," which launched them into another round of hysterics.

They laughed till their stomachs hurt, staggering around the clearing trying to catch their breath. They got pinned to the ground with laughter and had just about finished with it when Turk said, "At ease men," which started them laughing all over again.

When they were well and truly done laughing, Sydney sat up and said, "What about Shep? Poor guy. I wonder where he's hiding?"

They set out to search for him along the riverbank, calling out his name and listening for his whistle. After a while they got the sense that Shep wasn't anywhere nearby, and that he must have fled some distance away to escape Morton and his marauding troops.

As they walked back to the clearing, Turk turned to Sydney, "There's still one thing I don't get. How in the heck do you know where Morton lives?"

Sydney shook her head in dismay at her little brother and gave him a couple of knocks on his head. "Turk. Please. Think about it. I'm a witch!"

She walked on, leaving him there to ponder the matter. After a moment, understanding dawned on him and he ran to catch up with her. "Oh, I get it. It's another one of those candy lies—am I right?"

"More like a poison pill than a candy. It worked though, didn't it?"

They went back to Shep's place and Sydney left the remaining food and juice in the bag inside his house for him to find later, while Turk wandered around collecting the golf balls.

"Too bad we can't get any money for these things," he said, showing the golf balls to Sydney.

A look of astonished delight popped onto Sydney's face. "Wait a minute! We can too get money for these things. Turk, you are so smart you don't even know it. I can't believe I didn't think of that already. Come on!"

They set off on the trail beside the Rat River, heading north. They were retracing their steps in the direction they'd come from when they first arrived at The Royal Woods. As they hiked along the trail, Sydney explained what she had in mind. In the days before their mom got sick, and their dad stopped doing much of anything, he had been an avid golfer. One of the most fun things Sydney had ever done with her dad was to go with him when he went golfing. What she liked doing best of all was searching for the balls he accidentally but frequently hit into the trees—frankly, he was a terrible golfer—especially because Sydney was very good at finding lost balls, and often found other balls as well.

"I used to bring the extra ones I found to the pro shop after and they'd pay me fifty cents apiece for them. One time I made, like, six dollars!" Sydney said.

"Whoa!" Turk exclaimed. "We've already made, um . . . don't tell me." He shut his eyes to do the calculations. "One dollar and fifty cents!"

"Correct! And we haven't even started looking yet. It's like free money!"

There was no need for Sydney to tell him where they were going now. Turk remembered that one of the first places they'd come to after leaving the rail yard on the morning of their arrival was a golf course. A sign on the gate said, "The Rat River Golf and Country Club—members only." They'd climbed a fence and snuck across the golf course before discovering the Rat River. Now they quickened their pace, eager to get back to that golf course and find the rich pickings that must surely be laying there just waiting for them to collect.

⚜

One thing Sydney and Turk hadn't remembered was how far away the golf course was. The morning passed and they were still hiking along the trail when the steamy midday heat arrived. It felt as though they were trekking through a hot African jungle. Their pace slowed but they trudged forward, up and down and around the twists and hills on the narrow trail along the river. It had been a mistake to leave the rest of their juice at Shep's place, because by the time they reached the golf course, they were soaked with sweat and parched with thirst. They clambered up the riverbank and flung themselves down on a small shady hill that overlooked the course.

Despite their heat and thirst, they couldn't help but enjoy the view. It was a beautiful sight to behold. They hadn't paid much attention to the Rat River Golf and Country Club the first time they'd been there. It had been early in the morning then, and they'd been anxious to get to the farm, and so they'd slipped along the edge of the golf course trying not to be noticed. But now they took the time to really study the place.

The grass on the fairways was so lush and evenly trimmed it looked like a soft green carpet. Here and there, thick stands of huge old oak and elm trees created welcome pools of shade. The brilliant afternoon sun made the sand in the bunkers dazzle like diamonds, and turned the water ponds a sparkling sapphire blue. Every shade of green—from light almost white, to dark almost black—was featured in the pleasant curves and hills of the golf course. The rich smell of fresh cut grass mingled with the sweet aroma of the brilliantly coloured flowers that grew in abundance everywhere. Off in the distance, they could see the magnificent clubhouse. It looked like a luxurious old mansion, with walls of fieldstone painted white as snow, and all around it was a sprawling green-coloured wooden veranda.

"Wow," Turk said in awe. "I bet this is what heaven looks like."

"Probably," Sydney said, scrambling to her feet. "Let's go see if they've got anything to drink in heaven."

They walked in the shady rough beside the fairway and soon came to the place where the golfers tee off for the seventh hole. To their relief, they found a drinking fountain, and Sydney and Turk took turns guzzling fresh cold water and splashing themselves till they were both bloated and soaking wet.

Hearing the sound of some approaching golfers, they ducked behind the trees and hid.

Three white-haired men strolled toward the tee, the metal spikes of their golf shoes crunching loudly on the gravel path. The way they were dressed made Turk think of circus clowns. They wore black and white shoes with tassels on them, loud plaid pants, and neon bright shirts. Behind them followed three boys carrying their golf clubs. The boys were sweating and panting like dogs under the weight of the heavy bags, and they looked sullen and bored.

"Those are the caddies," Sydney whispered to Turk. "In a fancy-shmancy place like this, golfers get guys to carry their clubs for them."

As the three men took turns hitting their balls off the tee, Sydney quietly explained how the game works. "There's eighteen holes. See that, way down there, where that flag is? That's the hole. The smooth place all around it is called the green. First, you have to get your ball on the green. Then you have to putt it into the hole. There's different clubs for every shot. The less times you hit the ball, the better your score is. The guy who can get the ball into the hole with the fewest number of shots is the winner. It looks easy, but actually it isn't. Just ask Dad."

Just as she said that, one of the men took an awkward lurching swing at his ball and sent it curving into the trees off the fairway. "Shish-kebab!" he exclaimed, and the other two golfers chuckled.

"See what I mean?" Sydney said. "That's what you call a hacker. That'll be our first find of the day. Come on."

In fact, they never did find that ball, or many others for that matter. They spent the rest of that hot afternoon searching for balls in the trees and tall grass that edged the fairways. It turned out to be a much more difficult task than they'd expected. It was one thing to find balls just for fun, when she was out on the golf course with her dad on a relaxing Sunday afternoon. It was quite another to actually have to find balls to get money for food to eat. After three hours of diligent searching, they were woozy and cross-eyed from staring at the ground. Turk got three and Sydney had found only two. Turk was too weary to do the math, so Sydney did it for him.

"It comes to a grand total of eight golf balls, including the ones those goofs threw at us. That's, like, four lousy bucks," she grumbled.

Later that afternoon, they walked up to the grand front entrance of the clubhouse, but they couldn't gather the nerve to actually enter and try to sell their golf balls. The place looked so big and opulent, and they felt so small and wretched. They decided to come back tomorrow. Maybe then they'd have better luck searching for balls and be in a better mood to enter the clubhouse. All they wanted to do now was get back to their house. Besides, Kumar had invited them to eat at the gas bar, and they didn't want to risk missing him.

They trudged back to The Royal Woods along the trail, and didn't arrive at Shep's place until early evening. There was still no sign of him anywhere, and no one had touched the food they'd left in his shack. Seeing that gave them a very grim feeling indeed. Where had Shep gone? They were really starting to worry about him now.

Kumar's warm greeting at the gas bar came as a welcome relief at the end of such a hard day. He was delighted to see them, and invited them into the cool air-conditioned booth to join him for dinner. The delicious smell of spicy curry filled the little booth. Kumar had prepared a special meal for them. There were tasty samosas to start with—baked pastries with potato centres—followed by rice with chicken and vegetable curry, all served in shiny clean stainless steel metal containers, and washed down with ice-cold water and then some spicy Indian tea called chai. For dessert, Kumar served them delicious and unusual sweets. It was by far the best meal the two had eaten since arriving at The Royal Woods. Maybe the best meal they'd had in years.

While they ate, Kumar dealt with the customers gassing up their cars, and chatted pleasantly with Sydney and Turk. Sydney sat on a tall stool and Turk sat on the counter, right between the cash register and a religious shrine to the Hindu goddess Kali.

"By the way," Kumar eventually asked them, "where is your father today?"

"We don't know. We can't find him," Turk replied casually. "And anyway, he's not our real dad. We ran away from our real dad."

"Oh, brother," Sydney said.

CHAPTER SEVEN

WORKING FOR THE MAN

R an away?" Kumar asked calmly and not in the least bit surprised. "May I ask why?"

Sydney realized that she had no choice but to tell Kumar the truth. For one thing, she knew that Turk would not allow her to get away with yet another candy lie just for the sake of smoothing things over with Kumar. For another, she was in no mood to invent a story just then. But above all, the look of concern in Kumar's wise and sincere brown eyes made her incapable of being dishonest with him anymore. She felt sure that she could trust him, and that he would understand their situation.

Sydney sipped her chai and told Kumar everything— about how their mother had died and their father had gotten too sad to care for them. She explained that their main reason for leaving was so that their dad could get better and start a new life without them around to remind him of their mom.

Kumar had doubts about that. "As a father myself, I find it difficult to believe that having his two children run away might help him to feel better. Especially two such fine children as yourselves. So good and polite. Perhaps we should phone him, and discuss this matter?"

"No way, Kumar," Sydney said, shaking her head. "We've thought a lot about this. There's no turning back now. We've come way too far. Maybe someday we'll go home and visit him, just to say hello and make sure that he's okay and all. But not now. Not until we're all settled in here and we don't have to bother him about anything."

Kumar pondered Sydney's words with a grave expression on his face. "I am sorry Sydney, but I cannot accept that. I'm afraid something must be done."

"Does that mean you're going to call the cops?" Sydney asked, wincing.

"Oh no, I would never do such a thing. I am in no position to be making contact with the authorities at present. You see, Sydney, I have my own concerns in that regard. Since you have told me the truth about yourselves, I will tell you the truth about myself. The fact of the matter is, I am not supposed to be working in this country. It is not legal for me to be doing so. After some time here, maybe I am able to get the papers to stay and to work. And then I will bring my wife and children, who are living with such hardships now. Until that fine day, I must remain very quiet and careful."

Turk couldn't quite understand what Kumar meant by all of this, but figured that he'd get Sydney to explain it later. What he did understand though is that all three of them were living secret lives. This seemed like a good thing to him, because it meant that they were all in it together, along with Shep for that matter, since he was quite clearly an outlaw citizen of The Royal Woods.

Kumar studied them fondly for a moment. "As for you two, I will think about these things you have told me, and we must talk about it further. But now unfortunately there is no time. I must prepare to go to my next job. You will meet me in the morning, at the Chubby Princess?"

"For sure," Sydney said, climbing down from the stool she'd been sitting on to eat. "And thanks so much for dinner, it was yummy."

"Yeah, thanks Kumar," Turk said, jumping off the counter where he'd been sitting. "That was great. And don't worry about us. Really. We'll be okay."

Kumar smiled at Turk and patted him on the head. "I am certain that you will. But still, I do worry. I can't help but worry. And I want you to think very carefully about your father. We must decide about this matter of phoning him."

Sydney and Turk stepped out of the cool booth and into the soft, warm evening twilight. On the western horizon, the vast sky looked like a wild smear of butter on a big purple plate. As they walked past the gas pumps, Kumar poked his head out of the booth. "One moment please! Where will you be staying tonight?"

"Oh, we . . . uhm, rented a house not far from here. See you tomorrow!" Sydney replied breezily and then waved and walked on.

Kumar looked puzzled. "How is that possible?" he asked himself as he watched them trek across the big parking lot. "Such mysterious children."

Sydney wasn't angry at Turk for telling Kumar about their dad. In fact, she felt relieved that Kumar finally knew the truth about them. And Turk understood why Sydney had to tell the little candy lie about renting a house. Knowing that they were living in an empty house that they'd simply borrowed, without anyone's permission, would have only made Kumar even more worried. And Kumar seemed worried enough about them already.

Turk was in favour of Kumar's idea about phoning their dad though. It had only been three days since they'd last seen their dad, but Turk was already missing him a lot. He figured their dad might be starting to miss them too. Now that the idea had come up, Turk was desperate to talk to him on the phone, just to say hello and tell him that they were doing okay. Knowing how stubborn and determined Sydney could be, however, he realized that there was no point in saying anything about it to her right then. He felt confident though that soon enough, Kumar would persuade Sydney that it was the right thing to do. For now, he'd just have to be patient. In his usual quiet way, Turk thought all of these thoughts without saying a word.

They got back to their new house just before it turned dark. It felt like weeks since they'd been there. Even though the house was quiet and empty, and they'd only spent one night there, it truly did feel like home. Once inside with the door locked, they felt safe and secure. Sydney took a long hot bath, and Turk had a shower. Then they climbed into their sleeping bags in their separate bedrooms. "Good night!" Turk called out. "Good night!" came Sydney's reply from down the hall. For the second night in a row, they both enjoyed a long and delicious sleep in their spacious new house.

⁂

Sydney and Turk awoke early the next morning to a beautiful view of the crystal clear blue Manitoba sky right out their bedroom windows. They were both up and dressed and out the door within minutes, eager to start the day.

Kumar had a special breakfast ready for them that morning at the Chubby Princess.

"No more doughnuts for you two," he smiled. "You must be eating only real food from now on. There is no satisfaction for the body in eating doughnuts, no matter how many you consume. In fact, the more you eat, the less the satisfaction. Such is the science of doughnut marketing."

Sydney hesitated before taking the bag of food Kumar had ready. "You really shouldn't be doing this for us Kumar. You should save your money for your own kids," she said, feeling embarrassed and undeserving of all his generosity.

"This is a small thing, and it gives me much pleasure to help with your provisions. I can't tell you how much it means to me. Please, take it for my sake. And be on time for supper this evening, at the gas bar. We have important matters to discuss, as you know. Promise me that."

They promised to be there, said thanks, and made their way to Shep's place with the bag of food Kumar had prepared. When they got to the clearing, they were discouraged to find that there was still no sign of Shep. They sat down at the little pool table, somewhat forlornly, and ate the hard-boiled eggs, chapatti bread, carrot sticks, apples, and ice-cold mango juice that Kumar had packed for them. They both ate quietly, listening hard for the sound of Shep's whistling. But aside from the wind in the trees and the twittering little birds, the clearing rang with silence. Shep seemed to have vanished off the face of the earth. When they'd finished eating, there was more than enough food left over for their lunch, which Sydney tucked into her backpack—Turk had left his at the house—before they set off for the Rat River Golf and Country Club.

Being familiar with the route meant that the walk didn't seem quite so long this time. They hiked quickly along the trail and arrived by mid-morning. They approached the clubhouse through the parking lot, feeling much more sure of themselves than when they'd faced the prospect of entering that imposing building yesterday. Before they went in though, Turk had something he simply had to attend to.

"Hold on just a minute here," Turk said, in his most serious voice. He stood stock still in the middle of the parking lot, awestruck by all the big and exotic cars and SUVs gleaming and sparkling in the morning sun. Turk was a total car nut, and he knew the names of every vehicle in the lot. "Look at that. It's the brand new Stateside Super Trauma," he said pointing at a shiny silver SUV that looked so big you'd need a stepladder to get inside. "Oh my god! There's a Bavarian Alpine Guzzler," he said staring an even bigger silver vehicle. "And look! An Impervious Maximus. And a Sumo Surfer with the Tsunami Package!"

Sydney thought they all looked the same—big, stupid, and ugly—and she couldn't have named even one of them if her life depended on it. But she didn't want to spoil Turk's fun by saying as much. Besides which, it was sort of fun for her too, just watching her little brother charging around the parking lot exclaiming madly over these bright metal monsters. Turk looked so very small by comparison. It occurred to Sydney that this was the first time in days that she'd seen Turk truly enjoying himself, just being a little boy, passionately absorbed by something as silly as a bunch of shiny new cars. Sydney sat down on the curb and watched Turk have his fun.

When he was satisfied that he'd studied and identified every single vehicle in the parking lot, Turk made his way over to Sydney, shaking his head in awe. "So cool," he sighed.

Now at last they were ready to try their luck in the Rat River Golf and Country Club.

As impressive as the place was from outside, it was even grander on the inside. Entering from the blazing sunshine, through big wooden doors and into the luxurious clubhouse, it was all at once cool and dark and hushed. The rich red carpet in the wide entrance hallway was as thick and soft as a bed, and the ceiling was at least two stories high. As they passed the spacious dining room, they could hear the clink of cutlery, relaxed conversation and laughter, and they could smell the delicious aroma of fried bacon, brewed coffee, and fresh baked pastries.

"I smell strudel," Sydney said painfully, and wondered if it was too soon for them to eat the rest of their boiled eggs and carrot sticks.

At the end of the hallway they found the pro shop where the golf equipment and clothes were sold. "Excuse me sir," Sydney said to a small and friendly looking man behind the counter. The man's slick silver hair was styled into a big complicated wave, and he had tiny twinkling blue eyes and smelled powerfully of spicy cologne. It seemed to Sydney that everyone in this place wore permanent smiles and tons of cologne. "Are you the pro here?"

"Well if it isn't Rusty and Dusty," the man said, smiling merrily. "I sure am. The name's Chip Long. What can I do you for?"

Sydney had already explained to Turk that golf and country clubs always had an old professional golfer on hand to teach people how to golf and sell them clubs and things. Guys like Chip Long, for example.

"We found some golf balls we'd like to sell. You interested?" Sydney asked.

"Oh, a couple of business tycoons, eh? Sure, we can always use old golf balls for the practice range. Show me what you got there, Rusty," Chip said.

Sydney took eight golf balls out of her backpack and rolled them across the counter.

"Whoa. How much you need for them?" the old pro asked.

"For you Chip? Special price—seventy-five cents each," Sydney said.

"You drive a pretty hard bargain there kiddo. Tell you what, I'll give you ten bucks for the lot, not a penny less," Chip said, opening the cash register.

"Deal!" Sydney said, beaming. "We'll be back later today with some more, okay?"

"I'm looking forward to it," Chip said.

Turk and Sydney thanked him for the money and scurried out to the main hallway, barely able to contain their elation. It was only when they were well away from the pro shop that they stopped to celebrate, and even then they did so quietly, doing their secret handshake and snickering like a pair of thieves. Maybe this golf ball collecting idea was going to work out after all.

They walked through the front door of the clubhouse and onto the big veranda facing the golf course. In their excitement, they almost bumped right into a group of golfers who were just about to head out to the course. There were two men and two women in the group, and their caddies stood waiting for them at the bottom of the veranda stairs. The caddies were all teenaged boys with baseball caps on backwards, chewing gum, and looking bored.

As Sydney and Turk excused themselves and slipped around the golfers, they overheard one of the men complaining. "Where is that kid?" the man grumbled. "This is the third time this week he's been late."

"Can't you just get another one?" asked one of the women. She seemed to be the man's wife, because they both looked so much alike—streaked blond hair, baby-smooth sun-browned skin, smiling bright white teeth faces, and both tall and a little bit tubby.

"There's no other caddies available Barb," the man muttered at her through his pasted on smile.

Turk noticed that even though the man and woman never stopped smiling, there was an angry impatience simmering just beneath their happy expressions. It was strange to see two people who could keep right on smiling when they were both so obviously mad about something. But what made Turk really take notice of these two people is that he recognized them from somewhere. He just couldn't put his finger on where.

Sydney and Turk were about to step off the veranda when Sydney stopped and faced the group of golfers. "I'll be your caddy, sir," she announced in a clear and confident tone.

This took everyone by surprise. The group of golfers stopped talking and looked at her. The group of caddies stopped chewing gum and looked at her. And Turk stopped breathing and looked at her.

"Aren't you a bit too young to be a caddy? Not to mention, a bit too girl?" the man asked, still wearing that same tight smile that never seemed to leave his face.

The teenaged caddies all laughed.

"Maybe, but I've had tons of experience, sir," Sydney asserted.

Turk almost blurted out, "When?" But luckily, he didn't.

"Oh forget it, Bob," his wife said hurriedly. "Just take her. Mr. and Mrs. Crabstock are waiting," she said, turning her smiling hard face at the other couple.

The man directed his smile at Sydney. "Alright kid. Get the bag. Let's go."

And just like that, Sydney became a golf caddy.

She pushed her backpack into Turk's arms, skipped down the veranda stairs, and hoisted the big red golf bag onto her shoulder. She staggered around a bit under the weight of the bag until she found her balance. "Wait for me at Shep's place," she said with a wink to Turk, and then stumbled off to catch up with the other caddies who were already trudging toward the first tee. The two golfing couples were laughing and chattering away as they strode on ahead of them.

Everything happened so quickly that Turk was left standing there by himself, completely stunned by this astonishing turn of events. All he could do was stare dumbly at his sister as she set off on her bold new endeavour without him.

As you know, if you've been following their story closely, this was the first time since they'd hopped that train back East that Sydney and Turk were separated from each other. Finding himself alone didn't give Turk a very good feeling. What's more, he now remembered where he recognized that couple from, and that gave him an even worse feeling. Did Sydney realize who they were? Turk jogged after them to alert Sydney to his discovery. But he hesitated and slipped behind a tree when he saw that one of the golfers was already hitting her ball off the first tee. Turk kept his distance and watched while the other golfers drove their balls, after which the entire group marched off down the fairway like a small ragged parade. Sydney looked back at him once with a smile and a wave as if to say it's all okay. Turk waved back and watched them go.

Even though Sydney had told him to go wait for her at Shep's place, Turk had no intention of leaving the country club without her. He decided he'd do what the two of them had come there for in the first place—search for golf balls. He figured that if he stayed hidden in the rough, he could look for balls and follow Sydney at the same time. Maybe he'd even get the chance to tell her of his vital discovery. He was desperate to inform her about this, and worried that if she didn't know, something terrible might happen. He could not have said exactly what terrible thing might happen, but it gave him an awful feeling anyway.

As for her part, Sydney was concentrating too hard on doing her job to think about anything else. She didn't think about who the people she was caddying for were, or even notice that Turk was always lurking in the rough nearby as the group moved around the course. Sydney focused every bit of herself on being a good caddy.

All those times she'd gone golfing with her dad came in handy. Sydney always knew exactly what club was needed, where to stand when the golfers were hitting, and how to walk quietly on the green and not step in front of anyone's putt. She even thought to put a little towel over the clubs so they wouldn't clank noisily as she carried them down the fairway. And unlike the other caddies, who often had to be told to do things two or even three times, and seemed to sullenly resent their every duty, Sydney did her tasks quickly and politely, usually before she was even asked. Sydney never complained or lagged too far behind the golfers, and she never made a sound when the golfers were hitting. In fact, she didn't utter a single word to anyone during the entire eighteen holes of golf. Not only did the other caddies often talk and joke around and have to be told to keep quiet, but once, when one of the women golfers was putting, her caddy actually farted. Quite loudly, too.

Turk was waiting outside the clubhouse when the group finished their round of golf. He had found four more golf balls, sold them in the pro shop, and bought himself something cold to drink from a pop machine.

"Hey there Dusty, where's Rusty?" Chip Long asked Turk when he found him sitting by himself, crunching on a carrot stick and sipping his can of pop on a bench beside the caddy shack.

"Here she comes," Turk said, pointing to Sydney who was marching in with the group of golfers. She was looking straight at Turk with a sly grin on her face, and she didn't appear in the least bit tired. In fact, she was brimming with energy. The other caddies dragged along well behind them, looking as though they'd just run a marathon through a corn field.

"Well, what do you know. If it isn't Rusty," Chip said as the group arrived. "Got yourself a new caddy there, eh Big Bobby?" Chip said to the man who'd hired Sydney.

"The regular kid didn't show, so we used her instead," Bob replied, still smiling.

"How'd she work out?" Chip asked.

"No problems," Bob said. "At least she doesn't chew gum and whine all the time like these other characters. And she never farted either, at least I don't think she did."

Sydney blushed and Chip nodded and winked at her.

"Put our clubs in the car, would you, kid? It's the brand new silver Bavarian," Bob said, handing Sydney the keys with his smile and a crisp new twenty-dollar bill. "We want you here same time tomorrow. Don't be late. Leave my keys with Chip."

It's a good thing for Sydney that Turk was there. It would have taken her forever to find the right car, especially since almost every vehicle in the lot was silver. They walked out to the parking lot together, first carrying Bob's golf clubs and then returning for his wife Barb's. Sydney talked non-stop the entire time, describing each and every little thing that had happened, and how hard she'd tried to do a good job, and wasn't it great that she'd made twenty dollars and had another job tomorrow, because that meant they didn't have to worry about money anymore, and all their troubles were over. Turk nodded, keenly agreeing with her every word, waiting for an opening to jump in to tell her the news that he'd been bursting with all afternoon. But Sydney just kept chattering away, and it wasn't until they'd dumped the second set of clubs into the back of the SUV and slammed the door shut, that a brief second of silence allowed Turk to blurt out, "It's Bob and Barb Buick!"

"What?" Sydney asked.

"The people you're caddying for! It's Bob and Barb Buick!"

"And that matters because. . . ?" Sydney asked.

"That matters because Bob and Barb Buick are the people who are selling our house. Don't you remember? The sign? Out front? We're living in Bob and Barb Buick's house for Pete's sake," Turk said.

"Holy moly," Sydney said.

CHAPTER EIGHT

BUICK WORLD

Sydney and Turk didn't get a chance to discuss the matter any further right then. They walked back to the caddy shack in silence, while Sydney pondered what this news might mean. Was it a good or a bad thing? Or did it even matter? Turk, who'd been thinking it over all afternoon, had his own ideas on the subject, but he wanted to hear Sydney's point of view before he shared them.

"Feel up to going another round this afternoon there, Rusty?" Chip asked her when they arrived at the caddy shack and Sydney handed him the car keys.

Normally, she would have corrected Chip on this business of calling her Rusty all the time, but under the circumstances, Sydney thought it might not be bad idea to keep her real name a secret. Besides which, Chip was being pretty nice to them. And anyway, he seemed like the kind of guy who called everyone by nicknames, probably even his own mother.

"Sure," she said. "With pleasure."

"That a girl," Chip smiled. "Wish we had more caddies like you around here. You'll be caddying for old Doc Gamble. He'll be along any minute. And by the way, you better put on one of these. You too, Dusty," he said, handing them each an official Rat River Golf and Country Club golf cap. "You both look pretty much done in the sun."

Chip was right about that. All their adventures of the last few days had exposed them to plenty of sunshine, especially since their hats got blown off their heads almost as soon as they'd hopped that train back East. Turk was as brown as maple syrup, and Sydney's face had exploded with freckles, much to her dismay.

They thanked Chip and put on their new hats. As soon as Chip left, Turk drooped like a lost puppy. "Come on, Sydney," he moaned, "Let's get out of here. I've had enough of this place already."

"I know, Turk. I feel the same way. But we need the money, so I should do this while I've got the chance. Any minute now we could get kicked out of that house and have to go live someplace else. Money would sure come in handy if that happens."

"Heck," Turk cursed, but he didn't say anything more because he realized she was right. Still, it didn't give him a very good feeling to know that he'd be left on his own for the rest of the day. Sydney instructed him to look around for Shep a little bit, and then meet her back at the gas bar for dinner with Kumar. She'd think over what to do about Bob and Barb Buick, and they'd talk about it later. That was pretty much all she had time to say before Dr. Gamble and his golfing partners arrived. Sydney just barely got a chance to polish off Turk's pop, and then she was gone.

Turk decided to follow her advice this time. He didn't feel up to walking around searching in the rough for balls anymore, and it amazed him that Sydney still had it in her to haul a heavy bag of clubs for another eighteen holes of golf. It was yet more proof for Turk—as if he needed any more— that his sister had the strength and determination of a lioness.

Here's where our story splits in two, and it's hard to decide who we should follow—Turk or Sydney. It's probably best to follow Turk for now, since he had the more surprising experiences of the two. We'll rejoin Sydney later, just to see how she's making out.

Turk didn't put much effort into searching for Shep. In fact, he carefully avoided Shep's place altogether. He was already feeling pretty lonesome, and didn't want to end up feeling even worse if he discovered that Shep was still missing. Turk ambled along the trail by the river at a snail's pace, fooling around and exploring, just trying to kill the time until he could meet up with Sydney and Kumar for dinner at the gas bar. It was still far too early for that when he got back to The Royal Woods, so he thought maybe he'd go back to their house and have a little nap.

Unfortunately, almost as soon as he ventured into The Royal Woods, Turk got lost. He was having the same problem that they'd experienced the first time he and Sydney explored there in search of a place to live—all of the houses and streets looked the same. And, of course, there was no one around to ask for directions. He waved at a passing car to stop, but the people just waved back and drove on by. Knowing that their house was at the south end of The Royal Woods, Turk squinted up at the sun to determine the way. The sun was still high in the sky, and just beginning to slide toward the western horizon. Or does it slide toward the eastern horizon? And if the west is that way, is the south to the right or the left? Turk knew the correct answers to these questions, but he kept guessing that he must have it all wrong, and so he got himself turned around and around until he hardly knew which way was up anymore.

After a while, Turk found himself in a part of The Royal Woods he'd never been before. The houses were much bigger here. In fact, they were monstrously big, and all trying their very best to look like fairy-tale palaces in a picture book. Some of them were painted pink with gold trim, while others were baby blue with silver trim, and the front yards were crowded with water fountains and chalky white statues of naked athletes. Behind the houses was a little park that had a fake lake with a fountain gushing in the middle.

There were only a few skinny new trees in the park, so there was no shade for Turk to escape from the blazing hot sun. He looked around, trying to figure out what to do next. With no place to turn, he crawled under the lone picnic table in the park and sat there, eating the rest of the food Kumar had given them that morning. The mango juice was as warm as tea by then.

"What're you eating?" Turk heard a voice ask. He peeked out from under the table and, to his shock, there were the twins, Brad and Chad.

Turk didn't say a word at first. It wasn't that he was afraid of Brad and Chad—they seemed harmless enough—but that Morton character was another matter, especially without Sydney there to scare him off. Was Morton with them? Turk looked all about and was relieved to see that Morton was nowhere in sight.

"Carrot sticks. You want some? I've got exactly two left. I have to warn you, though, they're a tiny bit soft," Turk said.

"Bleechh!" Brad gagged in disgust. "That's gross. Hey kid, why don't you come to our place and have some pizza dogs?"

Turk slipped out from underneath the picnic table. The prospect of pizza dogs was tempting, but he wanted to make absolutely certain that Morton wasn't with them. Maybe this was a trap. He surveyed the open expanse of the park. There was no sign of Morton and no possible hiding places anywhere nearby.

"Where's your friend Morton today?" Turk asked, innocently.

"He's at baseball camp," Chad replied. "We're supposed to be at shopping mall camp but we had tummy aches so we got to stay home."

"Come on," said Brad, "let's go, I'm starving."

"Okay," Turk shrugged, and set off with Brad and Chad. They walked around the small fake lake in the middle of the park until the came to one of the big pink palace houses. They entered through a tall wooden gate into a backyard that featured a huge swimming pool brimming with balls and toys and all manner of floating devices. There were so many things in the pool you could hardly even see the water.

Turk followed Brad and Chad up onto the deck at the back of the house and through sliding glass doors into a massive sparkling clean white kitchen. The air conditioning must have been set on North Pole, because inside felt as cold as a Monday morning school day in January.

"Whew! That was some walk," Brad groaned. "I'm wiped."

Of course, Turk didn't say anything about that, but he couldn't help smiling a little. That was some walk? Over the past few days, Turk had probably walked about a hundred miles more than that. He slipped Sydney's backpack off his shoulder and tucked it in a corner, just to be ready for whatever happened next.

"Mira Bella!" Chad bellowed, "Pizza dogs! Now!"

"Who's Mira Bella?" Turk asked.

"She's our servant," Chad said.

Servant? Turk thought. Do these guys actually have a servant? As though in answer to his question, a tiny old Asian lady suddenly appeared in the kitchen.

"Pizza dogs. To the game room. On the double," Brad

ordered. "And make some fresh lemonade—plenty of ice and double the sugar."

The little woman nodded meekly and immediately began bustling about the kitchen. "Yes, my darlings," she said.

Turk followed the twins down a wide circular staircase to the game room. Like everything else about this house, the game room and all of the things in it were stupendously large. The TV screen was as big and flat as a highway billboard, the pool table looked like a football field, and the bowling lanes at the far end of the room seemed to stretch to infinity. Turk had never seen anything like it before. Not only did the room contain every imaginable game—from darts, to Ping-Pong, to table hockey, and even indoor golf—but there were mountains of toys as well, including at least two dozen remote control cars spilling out of a closet. More than anything, it was the sight of all those cars that really got to Turk. For as long as he could remember, Turk had craved a remote control car. It was impossible to believe that anyone could own this many of them. He would have liked to ask if he could try out just one, but the very sight of all those remote control cars had rendered him temporarily speechless.

Before Turk could collect himself to ask about trying out one of the cars, the big TV screen flashed on like a crack of lightning. "Want to play *Mall Monkey*?" Brad shouted over the roar of the video game. "Me first!" Chad howled.

The twins fought over the controller till Chad wrestled it away and began playing. The game featured an insane monkey crashing around inside a shopping mall. The monkey ate whatever merchandise it could grab as it raced from store to store, and the more it ate, the bigger it grew. Meanwhile, mall cops chased the monkey around, shooting at it with machine guns. The noise of the game was deafening. The gunfire boomed, the monkey screamed, and underneath it all, crazy loud dance music pounded out a frantic rhythm.

"Here is your snack time, my darlings!" Mira Bella shouted as she came down carrying a tray of pizza dogs and lemonade. She set the tray on a coffee table and disappeared. Chad dropped the controller and lunged for the pizza dogs right beside Brad. They knelt at the coffee table and went at the food as though it were an eating contest. It was a total frenzy. Turk waited till there was a brief lull in the action before he risked reaching in to pluck out a pizza dog, for fear that one of the twins might try to eat his hand.

"Hey, kid," Chad said. "Where'd you get that hat?"

"What hat?" Turk asked.

"The one on your head?" Brad said.

"Oh, that hat," Turk replied. He had completely forgotten that he was wearing the Rat River Golf and Country Club hat that Chip had given him. "Someone gave it to me. At the country club."

"Yeah? Our mom and dad are members there. They go golfing there every single day of the week," Chad said, through a mouth full of pizza.

"They sure must like golfing a lot," Turk observed.

"Not really," Brad said. "They actually hate it. They just do it so they can take people golfing and try to sell them houses. We own all the houses in The Royal Woods, you know. You must've seen the signs with their pictures all over the place. You know? Bob and Barb Buick? We're super rich, you know."

On hearing that, Turk gagged on the sip of lemonade that was half down his throat. He coughed and choked, and the twins stopped eating for a moment to see if Turk was going to drop to the floor and die.

"Sorry," Turk gasped, struggling to catch his breath. "I swallowed an ice cube."

It was all too incredible to believe. First Sydney gets a job caddying for Bob and Barb Buick, and then, later that same day, Turk finds himself eating pizza dogs in their very house with their twin sons, Chad and Brad. What next? Sydney falls in love with one of the twins and gets married?

Despite his astonishment, Turk did a pretty good job of keeping his cool—at least after he got over his initial near-death choking on lemonade experience. As usual, Turk stayed quiet, just thinking things over while he slowly ate his pizza dog. It wasn't long before it occurred to him that there was something very valuable he might be able to find out from the twins.

"How did your mom and dad end up owning all these houses anyway?" Turk asked.

"I dunno," Brad replied. "They bought 'em, I guess. We're super rich you know."

"No, you idiot," Chad interjected, spraying bits of pizza dog everywhere. "They didn't buy them—they built them. They bought the land, and then they got the houses built."

"Who'd they buy the land off of?" Turk asked.

"I dunno, some stupid old dirtbag farmer. They probably paid him about twenty-five bucks," Chad said, through a grinning mouth full of food.

"But where'd the farmer go?" Turk asked, his voice rising.

"Jeez, kid," Chad replied, "you sure ask a lot of dumb questions. How should I know? Wherever it is that stupid old dirtbag farmers go. Probably some dumpy shack somewheres."

"Some dumpy shack where?" Turk demanded, his voice becoming shrill.

The twins briefly stopped eating and looked curiously at Turk. They were surprised to see that he was on the verge of crying.

"Kid. Take it easy," Brad said. "It's just some stupid old dirtbag farmer. He's probably dead in a ditch by now."

"He is *not* dead in a ditch by now! And he is *not* a stupid old dirt bag farmer!" Turk raged. By now, he really was crying. Even Turk was surprised by that. He jumped up, blinded by the tears that flashed in his eyes. He had to get out of there before he went completely mental.

Without another word, Turk sprinted up the stairs, through the kitchen and out onto the deck. He ran at full speed, as though trying to run right out of his own tears. He was out of the backyard and all the way to the far side of the little park before he suddenly remembered something—he'd left Sydney's backpack in the kitchen. He slowed to a halt and bent over to catch his breath and wipe the tears from his face. What a humiliating experience that had been, and now he had to figure out what to do about that stupid backpack.

At first, Turk considered just leaving it there. But then maybe Sydney would kill him for losing it. He just couldn't stomach the idea of going back to that house and facing those twins again though. Not after what had just happened. Maybe Sydney would be willing to sneak in there and get it later? Or would she be so mad at him that she'd make him do it? Unfortunately for Turk, the simple truth of the matter was that he could have just walked away and left it. If Sydney knew what had happened, she wouldn't have been bothered about it at all. She'd have told him to forget the whole deal, and they could think about getting another backpack some other day.

It's too bad that Sydney wasn't there to tell him that, because after a wandering around the park for a while, brooding about the backpack, there was Turk, sneaking through the Buick's backyard and creeping up the deck stairs. He peeked through the sliding glass doors into the kitchen. There was the backpack, sitting in the corner right where he'd left it. And there, just a few steps away, was Morton, swaggering around the kitchen in a Yankees baseball uniform.

Turk spun away from the doors and pinned himself to the wall. What was Morton doing there? Baseball camp must have ended and he'd dropped by to boss the twins around for the rest of the day. Turk figured all he could do was wait till Morton and the twins left the kitchen, and hope that they didn't decide to come outside for a swim in

the pool. It was a perfect afternoon for a swim. But probably, Turk calculated, Morton would want to go to the
Game Room for some pizza dogs and to relax with a nice
game of *Mall Monkey*.

Turk listened hard, and could just barely make out the
sound of Morton talking to the twins, boasting wildly
about his exploits at baseball camp that day. "Dudes! I hit
seven home runs, including three grand slams. And I
pitched two no-hitters, all before lunch time."

It must be one of those fantasy baseball camps, Turk
figured.

It was a good thing for Turk that he could hear them
talking, because that's how he'd know when they left the
kitchen. After a while, the sound of Morton's bragging
faded and the kitchen fell silent. Turk waited an extra few
moments, just to make sure that they were really gone. By
the time he risked taking a peek inside the kitchen, it
seemed to Turk that he'd been waiting there for hours,
even though it had probably only been about ten seconds.

Satisfied that the kitchen was empty, Turk slid the glass
door open a crack. The booming roar of the *Mall Monkey*
game splashed over him like a wave. Turk held his breath,
slipped inside and made his way to the backpack. To avoid
making even the slightest disturbance, his every move was
slow and deliberate. He had the backpack over his shoulder
and was just turning to leave when the sound of a toilet
flushing froze him in his tracks. A door in the hall swung
open and there was Morton, pulling up his pinstriped

Yankee pants and loudly singing "Take Me out to the Ball Game."

It's safe to say that Morton experienced the bigger shock of the two. One glimpse of Turk, and Morton let out a scream that sounded exactly like the monkey in the video game. It probably flashed through his mind that Sydney must also be there, making good on her claim that she knew where they lived. Turk wasn't thinking about what was on Morton's mind, though. He was too busy hightailing it back the way he came, out the sliding doors, off the deck, through the yard and into the park.

Brad and Chad raced up from the game room to see what the commotion was all about.

"The red witch! She was here! In your house!" Morton yelled.

"Who?" asked Chad in confusion.

"The red witch from the river, don't you remember? By the bird man's shack! I just seen her! Well, not her exactly, but her little brother. He was right in the kitchen when I finished doing my poo poo!"

"No, it was just him. The little kid. She's not around," Chad explained urgently.

"How would you know?" Morton asked.

Chad was stumped for an answer. He couldn't dare tell Morton that they'd invited Turk into their house for snacks. Morton would be outraged if he knew they'd been consorting with the enemy. Chad abruptly changed the subject. "Let's go chase him!"

"Come on, men!" Morton barked. "Follow me!"

They got to the gate at the backyard just in time to catch a glimpse of Turk running out of the park in the general direction of the Rat River.

"He's headed for the river!" Morton bellowed. And the chase was on.

Meanwhile, back at the Rat River Golf and Country Club, Sydney was having a no less trying if not quite as exciting time of it herself. It turned out that the man she was caddying for wasn't called Dr. Gamble for nothing. There were three other golfers in the group, all of them doctors. One was a foot doctor, one was an ear, nose and throat doctor, and one was an eye doctor. Dr. Gamble was a brain doctor. The four doctors made bets on every hole and indeed, on every shot.

"I'll bet you a loonie you don't make it on to the green from here," the eye doctor would say to the ear, nose and throat doctor. Next it would be the foot doctor's turn. "I'll bet you a toonie you can't hit it over the river," he'd say to Dr. Gamble.

And so it went, for the entire eighteen holes. Because there was so much betting going on, Dr. Gamble told Sydney to secretly keep score for all of them, just to make sure nobody cheated. By the time the game was finished, Sydney was practically delirious from adding up all those numbers, not to mention from carrying golf clubs around for thirty-six holes. Lucky for her though, Dr. Gamble was the big winner on the day, because after he paid her twenty dollars, he asked her what she wanted as a tip.

"You're my lucky charm, Rusty. From now on I want you to be my regular caddy. Now then, what do you need for a tip?" the old doctor asked.

"Well, if it's okay with you, how about a couple of golf balls? My little brother collects them," Sydney said. To her amazement, Dr. Gamble gave Sydney six brand new golf balls and an extra ten dollars.

Sydney could not have felt happier as she made her way down the riverbank trail to The Royal Woods. Everything was working out much better than she could have possibly predicted only three days ago, when they'd arrived to the horrible discovery that the farm was gone. Despite everything, they now had a nice place to live, Sydney had found a well-paying job, and they even had a couple of good friends in the neighbourhood. For the moment at least, Sydney had no worries and nothing to look forward to except another delicious meal with Kumar, followed by a good night's sleep in their luxurious new house.

Even though she was exhausted from her long hard day of work, Sydney's happiness charged her with energy, so much so that she started to skip down the trail singing her favourite Avril Lavigne song. She didn't want to keep Turk and Kumar waiting.

Sydney's happy mood was short-lived though. She got to the gas bar right on time for dinner, but was alarmed to find that Turk wasn't there.

"I have not seen him all day. Where have you been?" Kumar asked when she came to the door of the booth.

"I'll tell you all about it later. I've got to find Turk. He's probably waiting at the house. We'll be right back!" Sydney called out over her shoulder as she set off running to the house.

But Turk wasn't at the house either, and Sydney could tell he hadn't been back since that morning. Everything was just as they'd left it. Her last hope was Shep's place. She sprinted toward the trail by the river, but all at once her energy drained away and she was practically crawling by the time she got to the little clearing. Shep's shack sat there, looking forlorn and abandoned, and there wasn't a soul around. Sydney flung herself to the ground in despair.

She didn't know whether to be mad or worried about Turk. The more she lay there thinking about it though, the more she realized that it was not like Turk to just disappear for no reason. Any anger she felt about him was soon over-whelmed by a wave of panic. She could have cried, but resisted the urge. Crying wouldn't do her any good now. What's more, it didn't seem right to cry about something that was all her fault. Why had she sent Turk off to wander around by himself? If he was lost in The Royal Woods, how would she ever be able to find him before dark?

Sydney decided that she had no choice but to retrace her steps. She dragged herself up, and stumbled off toward the Rat River Golf and Country Club. Maybe Turk had gone back there to find her.

CHAPTER NINE

BATTER UP!

You've no doubt played hide-and-seek plenty of times, so you know what thrilling fun that can be. Especially when you're the one being hunted. Your heart races and all of your senses go on high alert as you scramble from one hiding place to the next, trying to elude the one who is "it." And when you find a good spot to hide, you try to make yourself as small as a mouse, and stay as still and quiet as possible. There is nothing more hilarious than to sit holed up in a good hiding spot, watching your friends bumbling around hopelessly searching for you. It's as though you're invisible, and the only thing that can betray you is the sound of your own beating heart.

Turk was experiencing all of these sensations—the thrill of the chase, the mad dash from one hiding place to the next, his senses alert and electrified, the wild pounding of his heart as he hid, still and quiet, while the three boys hunted him. Except he wasn't finding any of this fun, and it certainly wasn't hilarious. That's because it didn't feel like a game.

Turk knelt in the muck at the edge of the Rat River, hidden under the cover of some low dense bushes. Peering up through the leaves, he had a tiny glimpse of the trail above. He could see and hear Morton and the twins, their white running shoes flashing past just a few feet away. They scurried this way and that, calling out to each other, and making occasional screaming forays into the bush on either side of the trail. They'd yell and thrash and poke at the bushes with long sticks, and then run to another spot and try there. It wasn't long before Turk realized that they were working a circle around him. And the circle was getting smaller and smaller. He gathered himself up like a spring, ready to explode out and flee if they got too close. Or maybe they were too close already. Maybe it was too late for him to make his move.

The chase had started all the way back in the park behind the twins' house. Turk hadn't even realized he was being chased at first. He still had no idea where he was in The Royal Woods, so he decided to make his way back to the Rat River. At least he knew where that was. With any luck, he'd meet up with Sydney on her way home from the golf course. It was a good thing Turk kept running after he'd left the Buick's backyard, because just as he got to of the far side of the park, he glanced back over his shoulder and saw that Morton was leading the charge with the twins in tow, heading straight for him. Turk didn't stop to ask what they wanted. He put his feet in high gear and took off running at double the speed.

Turk was quick and he had a good lead on them. He would have easily gotten away, especially since the twins weren't very fast runners, and Morton had to keep slowing down to yell at them. Unfortunately for Turk though, the first street that looked like it might lead to the river turned out to be a bay—a street that makes a small and pointless U—so that when he ran down that way, it took him right around to the street he'd just come from, right in time to meet up with Morton and the twins.

They had slowed to a lazy trot by then, and were probably about to abandon the chase altogether. But when Turk suddenly reappeared, the chase was on again. Turk almost jumped out of his skin when he saw them. As you know, nothing makes you run faster than fear, and Turk is a pretty fast runner to begin with. He quickly outpaced them and was well away when he finally found a route into the trees along the riverbank.

The problem was, Turk couldn't find the river trail. Crashing through the thick bush slowed him down considerably, and he kept tripping over fallen trees and branches, and getting caught and torn up by vicious thorns and giant weeds. Carrying that backpack wasn't helping matters either. The harder he pushed to go fast, the more he stumbled and fell. He began to panic, which only made things worse. Out of desperation, he'd sprint toward any small clearing he saw and thus lost all sense of direction. If only he could find the trail. Then he could really open up and be long gone. But he was confused by panic and blinded by the dense brush, so he couldn't find his way.

Morton and the twins marched after him, their pace slow and methodical. In that way, they were easily able to gain on Turk. They followed the sight and sound of Turk's frenzied thrashing flight through the woods. They were carrying big sticks with which they whipped the trees, chanting "Smell the blood! Smell the blood! Smell the blood!"

Three times Turk stopped and hid from them. And three times he had to jump up and run when they flushed him out. Finally he stumbled onto the river trail, but by then Morton and the twins were right behind him, so he only managed to make it around a corner and down a hill before he had to deke off the path and hide again.

So there he was—hiding in the swampy bush by the river's edge while Morton and the twins searched the trail just above him. He hoped they'd think he had kept running down the trail, and then carry right on past him. But they were wise to that ruse. They circled back again and again, and now they were closing in on him. Turk was sickened by the sudden realization that Morton had spotted his tracks in the mud. That's when he knew it was time to go.

Turk took his eyes off the trail and studied the edge of the river for a possible escape route. There he saw a surprising but familiar sight. The big bent-over tree with the tire swing was only about thirty yards away.

Seeing that tree, Turk remembered an afternoon during the summer on the farm, when he and Sydney had been playing one of their regular games of hide-and-go-seek. It seemed like a lifetime ago now. On those fun and lazy hot afternoons, Turk would hide in some obvious spot while Sydney hunted for him, calling out his name and pretending not to know where he was. After a bit, Turk would leap out of his hiding place, and Sydney would feign amazement that he'd been hiding there all along. But once, he'd climbed up that big tree and tucked himself between the trunk and the limb that bent out over the river. Sydney really couldn't find him that time. Turk sat up there, trembling with excitement, listening to Sydney calling out his name and searching for him in all his usual hiding spots. He stayed up there for a long time, even after he could hear that Sydney was becoming desperate. She called for him again and again, till her voice was hoarse and frantic. It wasn't that Turk wanted to upset her, but he just couldn't give up this perfect hiding spot. It was way too much fun to be in a hiding place that she truly could not find. It wasn't until Sydney was almost in tears and wading right into the river, terrified that Turk had fallen in and drowned, that he chirped, "Here I am!"

Sydney was so happy to find him that she really did start to cry then, but she was mad too, so even though she was crying, she was also giving him heck and sort of laughing, all at the same time. Turk thought that his sister Sydney must be the only person in the world who could cry and laugh and be mad at him all at once.

Now Turk was calculating if he could make his way over to the tree and climb up into that perfect hiding spot again. He studied the route between the tree and his place in the bushes. It was rough and muddy, and thick with wicked weeds. It would be hard for him to scoot through all that without falling into the river or, worse still, getting spotted by the hunters. But Turk decided he could do it. And in fact he had to do it, now that Morton was sniffing around his tracks in the mud. He waited until Morton and the twins were far enough away, then he made his move.

Turk stayed low to the ground and scrambled over to the big tree. It felt good to be moving again. A rush of adrenalin propelled him through the swampy terrain, and he was at the base of the tree and then up on the limb within seconds. He curled up on the limb and hugged the big trunk, amazed that he'd accomplished the task so easily.

Something was different from the last time he'd been up there though. Turk had grown. He was only six that time he'd been up there hiding from Sydney, and now he was eight. His feet and arms stuck out the sides, making him clearly visible from the trail. If Morton or one of the twins happened to look up at the tree, they would spot him instantly. Hopefully, they wouldn't look. But there was another problem too. The mosquitoes, which had been annoying presence all through this long ordeal, were now unbearable. It was almost dusk, which is when the mosquitoes take ownership of the Rat River, and if you go down there then, it's just like you're visiting their place to deliver your blood for dinner.

It was impossible for Turk to keep still. Every few seconds he had to swat at the mosquitoes that were attacking him everywhere all at once. He fidgeted and squirmed, and twice he almost fell out of the tree trying to battle them off. They were driving Turk so crazy that he almost forgot why he was sitting up there in the first place.

It wasn't long before the inevitable happened.

"There he is! I found him! I found him!" Chad squealed in excitement, as though he'd just won an all-expense paid trip to Disneyland.

Chad was standing at the bottom of the tree pointing triumphantly up at Turk when Brad and Morton ran over, panting and sweating.

"So. We meet again," Morton said, grinning cruelly up at Turk. "We're taking you prisoner kid. You have the right to remain silent. Anything you say, can and will be used against you in a court of law. Now get out of the tree. We're putting you on trial."

"What for?" Turk asked miserably.

"For entering the Buick residence without proper authorization," Morton replied.

"They invited me to. They gave me a pizza dog. They asked me, and I said okay. I only had one pizza dog. I'll pay them back."

Morton spun around to glare at the twins. "What the...? Is this true?"

Brad and Chad glanced at each other sheepishly. "We gave him half a pizza dog in the park," Chad explained, "because he begged us for it. But then he must've snuck in to steal all the rest of our pizza dogs. We never invited him."

"That's not true!" Turk protested.

"Tell it to the judge," Morton concluded. "Get out of the tree. Now!"

"Who's the judge?" Turk asked.

"Me," Morton said. "If found guilty, you will be tied to a tree and whipped five times and left there till the mosquitoes drink all your blood." The whole time this discussion went on, all of them were hopping around, swatting off mosquitoes.

"Do I get a lawyer?" Turk asked, imagining that Sydney could mount an excellent defence in this case.

"If you need an attorney, the court will appoint one. You can have your choice of either Chad or Brad. Now get out of the tree. And I mean RIGHT NOW!" Morton yelled.

Turk didn't think he stood much of a chance of being found not guilty at such a trial. He decided to exercise his right to remain silent and stay in the tree. If he could sit up there long enough, he figured that the mosquitoes would eventually drive them away, or else the twins would want to go home and eat.

What Turk hadn't figured on was Morton's determination and meanness. There was no way that Morton was going to give up now. After much discussion and barking at the twins about not abandoning their duties—the mosquitoes were feasting on their chubby flesh, and they sincerely begged his permission to go home for supper—Morton decided it was time to take the prisoner by force. To Turk's horror, Morton started shinnying up the tree. He struggled and grunted his way up the trunk, and at one point, his face came so close that Turk could smell his sour stinky breath. The only thing Turk could do then was to go out further on the limb, out toward the tire swing. Turk straddled the limb like a horse, facing back at Morton, and pushed himself all the way out to the end. Any further and he'd fall into the river.

"Stick!" Morton ordered when he finally managed to get up on the limb. Brad reached up and handed him the longest stick in their arsenal. Morton turned himself around and straddled the limb to face Turk. He noodled his way out toward him, brandishing the stick like a whip. Turk looked down at the river, his only remaining escape route. He could drop out of the tree into the river and swim across to the other side. There would be no way for Morton to follow him unless he went into the river too, and Turk didn't think Morton would want to get his nice Yankee uniform all wet and muddy. But jumping into that river was not a very appealing prospect. Probably since the beginning of time, not one single person had ever willingly jumped into the Rat River. It was slow-moving and shallow and full of leeches, and the water was the colour of caramel candy. If he got stuck in the mud at the bottom of the river, would Morton or the twins even bother to rescue him? Turk cleared his mind of all these thoughts, and readied himself to let go of the tree and plunge in. He closed his eyes and was just about to do it when—

"Hey, Morton! Batter up!" And there was Sydney, a few yards away on the trail, winding up like a major league baseball pitcher. She was a left-hander with a sidearm throwing style, and she delivered her first golf ball pitch just inches from Morton's chin.

"High and inside! Ball one!" Sydney called.

"Hey!" Morton screamed. "Whatchadoing!? Don't! Hey! Help! Brad and Chad! Help! Help!"

Unfortunately for Morton, Brad and Chad were already well on their way home, having fled in terror the second they spotted Sydney running down the trail in their direction.

"A Yankee, eh Morty?" Sydney said, commenting on Morton's baseball uniform. "It figures. I've always hated the Yankees. Listen, I really gotta work on my fastball. I've been having some control problems lately."

She reached into her pants pocket and pulled out another one of the golf balls that Dr. Gamble had given her for Turk. She wound up and pitched another sidearm fastball. "Strike! That one was right down the old pipe, Morton. The count is one and one."

"What're you doing? You're crazy! You're gonna kill me!" Morton sobbed.

"No, I won't. Not if you can hit it, Yankee boy. Get that bat up there. Let's see your swing," Sydney taunted. "If you can hit a pitch, I'll let you run all the way home."

"Don't, Sydney," Turk said, "just let him go."

"Not till I get a look at his swing. Batter up, Morton!"

Sydney went into another windup, and Morton had no choice but to bring his stick up like a bat and try to connect with the next incoming golf ball. It was another fastball strike, and Morton swung wildly and missed.

"Strike two! Choke up on that bat, Morty. You swing like a girl," Sydney advised him.

Sydney's next pitch was high and away, and Morton made the mistake of going after it with another wild lurching swing. It was a mistake because it caused him to reach way out in front of him, which caused him to lose his balance, which caused him to topple off the tree limb and fall face first into the Rat River.

Turk was mortified. He almost dropped into the river to save him. But Sydney had a somewhat different reaction. She doubled over with laughter. She was in hysterics as she staggered down to the riverside for a better view of Morton floundering around in the mucky water. Morton clawed his way out of the river and sprawled on the bank like a big dirty catfish. He was drenched in wet mud from head to toe. He struggled to his feet, but then flopped backwards into the river again. Even Turk couldn't help laughing at that, and it just about killed Sydney.

"There is no joy in Mudville," she sputtered laughing. "Mighty Morton has struck out!"

Morton managed to get back out of the river and slither a little way up the bank. He stood up and put on his mud-soaked baseball hat with all the dignity he could muster. Then he huffed away, dripping water and muttering curses, his running shoes making squishing fart noises with every step.

When he was a safe distance away, Morton turned and yelled, "I'll get you for this! Vengeance is the name of my game!"

"Well baseball sure isn't the name of your game, Morton! You suck and so do the Yankees!" Sydney called after him, taking a couple of strides in his direction. When Morton saw Sydney moving toward him, he turned and took off running and never looked back.

With the long ordeal finally over and able to relax for the first time in hours, Turk stretched out on the limb with his arms and legs dangling down, dazed with relief that Sydney had arrived just in time to save him from going into the river. He sighed and sprawled there, grinning at her.

"You know what's really weird?" Sydney asked.

"No. What?"

"I was just thinking about you up in that tree. I was running around everywhere looking for you, and I was just coming back down the trail from the country club and I all of a sudden started seeing you up in that tree. Remember that time? When you were little and you went up there and hid from me and I got all mad at you?"

"Yeah," Turk said. "I remember."

"The weird thing is, all of a sudden I knew you were up there. I just knew it. I ran straight here looking for you. Weird, eh?"

"Yeah. Weird."

"Seriously. Do you think maybe I am a witch?"

"Probably," Turk said. "Yeah, for sure."

"A good witch or a bad witch?"

Turk had to think about that. "A bit of both," he concluded.

Turk looked at her for a moment, not smiling anymore,

just looking at his sister Sydney and thinking about how no brother anywhere had ever had a better sister than her. "Can we go get something to eat?" he asked. "I'm starving."

⁂

They were too late for dinner with Kumar at the gas bar. They went by there anyway, just in case he was working late, but he'd already left for his nighttime job. He'd be worried about them, they knew, but they'd just have to explain it all to him tomorrow morning, when they went for breakfast at the Chubby Princess.

They ate at the food court in the mall. Sydney said it was Turk's choice, and that they'd eat whatever he wanted. "Even burgers and shakes at Mad Scottish Clown Burger?" Turk asked.

"Sure. Why not?" Sydney said, even though she'd always claimed that their food was made from cardboard and cow poo.

There was a lot to talk about, so they sat in the food court long after they'd finished eating, discussing the events of the day. Of course Sydney was astonished to find out that Brad and Chad were the twin sons of Bob and Barb Buick, and that Turk had actually been inside their house eating pizza dogs. Turk told her how he figured the next surprising thing would be when she ended up falling in love with one of the twins and getting married. Sydney promised that there was no danger of that happening.

Sydney was especially impressed that Turk had tried to get information from the twins about Uncle Frank and Aunt Lily.

"I got the exact same idea about Bob and Barb Buick!" Sydney exclaimed. "That's why it's so great that I get to caddy for them every day. As soon I get to know them a bit better, I'll get them to tell me about the farm. You know what? We're actually going to find Uncle Frank and Aunt Lily now. To tell you the truth, I honestly never thought we would, but now I know for sure we will."

They bought some laundry soap in the mall and then headed back to the house. They'd only brought one change of clothes with them, and they badly needed a wash. "Unless you want to use the car wash again," Sydney teased.

"No thanks," Turk said.

"We've got to buy you some new clothes too. You got your shirt and pants torn up from all that fun playing hide-and-go-seek with your friends."

"I wasn't playing, it wasn't fun, and they're not my friends," Turk said.

"Just kidding," Sydney said, putting her arm around him. "Listen, that'll never happen again—promise. From now on, we always stick together. Always."

"Agreed," Turk said. And then they did their secret hand shake—two snaps, two slaps, and one palm slide.

Back at the house, Sydney figured out how to work the washing machine and dryer in the basement and got all their clothes as clean as new. Then they both got washed up and ready for bed. It had been an unbelievably long and arduous day. Tomorrow could only be easier, of that Sydney was certain. She would work hard, make lots of money and, with any lucky, find out about Uncle Frank and Aunt Lily.

Sydney tucked Turk into his sleeping bag and told him how proud she was of him, that he was the best and smartest and bravest boy in the world, and that now everything was going to get better. It wouldn't be long now before they'd find Uncle Frank and Aunt Lily. Turk curled up and listened, and then he asked her if she would sing him a song to put him to sleep. She couldn't think of anything to sing, but then she remembered the words to "Home on the Range." After she finished singing that old cowboy song, Turk lay there breathing deeply with his eyes closed. Thinking that he was asleep, Sydney quietly got up to leave.

"Sydney?" Turk asked drowsily, just as she got to the door. "There's one thing I've been wanting to ask you ever since we got here."

"What's that, Turk?"

"Can we go home now?"

CHAPTER TEN

A GHOST IN THE HOUSE

A strange thing happened at the Chubby Princess Doughnut Cottage the next morning. Turk arrived first. The sky was a pale dawn blue when Turk sprang out of his sleeping bag and woke up Sydney. Or at least he tried to wake her up. Sydney was so spent from all her endeavours of the previous day that she lay there like a rock, barely able to even pry open one eye. She stayed curled up in a motionless heap on the floor, while Turk danced around, urging her to get up. Finally he said, "Better get up or you'll be late for work! I'll see you at the doughnut shop. Bye bye!"

And off he sped. He ran the whole way there and skipped merrily through the door of the Chubby Princess. Kumar, who'd been worried sick about the both of them, was of course relieved and overjoyed to see Turk. All in a rush, Turk explained why they hadn't made it to the gas bar for dinner the previous evening. He told Kumar about Sydney's new job at the golf course, described the Buick's big pink mansion, recounted his terrifying ordeal on the riverbank, and ended by telling how Sydney had come along at the last possible second to save his life. In between serving his customers, Kumar listened attentively, reacting with joy, amazement, horror, and amusement to every turn of the story.

And then Sydney arrived, all bleary-eyed and looking weary and wary. Unlike Turk, Sydney had not been eager to meet with Kumar that morning. In fact she was dreading it. She was sure that Kumar was going to make them phone their dad immediately, which meant that they'd soon be on their way back home. And just when they'd finally gotten their new life in The Royal Woods all sorted out.

The night before, after Turk had asked her about going home, they talked and talked until they were both too tired to talk anymore. By the time they finally collapsed into their sleeping bags, Sydney had convinced Turk that they needed to stay in The Royal Woods for at least a little while longer. For one thing, they'd need money if they wanted to ride on the *inside* of the train for the journey home. (Neither of them was especially keen on riding the rails again.) She would have to do some serious caddying and he would have to find at least one hundred golf balls if they were to make enough money to buy train tickets. But more importantly, they were so very close to finding Uncle Frank and Aunt Lily. After all they'd been through, how could they even think about giving up now?

Turk agreed with Sydney on those points. He also acknowledged that they'd vowed to never go home or even mention the idea, and that deal had been sealed with their secret handshake. Although as Turk pointed out, that was before they knew the farm was gone. And so after much discussion, they reached a compromise. They would stay in The Royal Woods until they found Uncle Frank and Aunt Lily, or else until they saved enough money to go home— whichever came first. But in the meantime, Sydney agreed to let Kumar decide about phoning their dad. Secretly, Sydney resolved to think of some way to prevent that phone call from ever happening.

To Sydney's alarm, Turk and Kumar were already discussing the matter when she arrived at the doughnut shop, and she had yet to think of a way to talk them out of it. That's when Kumar said something that neither Sydney or Turk could have possibly predicted. This was the strange thing that happened at the Chubby Princess that morning.

"Last night I had a dream about your father," Kumar said, with his warm brown eyes gazing out the window. "In truth, it was more than a dream. It was in fact, a vision. I feel now like I have spoken with your father, and that I know him very well. I understand those things that went wrong in your home, and made you to run away. He is filled with such regrets. He wants a chance to start afresh, especially with you, Sydney. It made me to realize that everything will soon be okay, and that I no longer have to fret all my days and nights about you two. Soon you will be reunited with your dad. Of this, I am certain. In conclusion, there is no need of phoning him now."

"No need of phoning him now?" Turk asked in disbelief.

Seeing Turk's distress, Kumar reached across the counter and put a gentle hand on his shoulder. "Please. You must trust me now. Soon you will understand why. Everything will be well, Turk, I promise you."

Turk was baffled by Kumar's strange words. He had so many questions that he didn't know where to begin, and so he said nothing. Of course Sydney was hugely relieved that they weren't going to be forced to make that phone call. And she hadn't needed to conjure up even one single candy lie. Not wanting to gloat over her victory though, Sydney was careful to conceal her joy.

"It's going to be okay, Turk," she said, putting an arm around him. "You'll see."

Turk spun away from her arm, and stood there silently sulking.

Kumar looked at the two children—one sad and heavy with disappointment, the other happy and radiant with independence. Very soon, he thought and hoped, they will both be equally happy. As you will see, Kumar was trying his best to do the right thing here. But it was a very difficult thing for him to do.

Kumar had prepared another bag of food, and as he handed it to them he studied Turk, who stood staring glumly at the floor. "Please, miss. Promise to take good care of your brother, won't you?" Kumar said to Sydney.

"For sure," Sydney said smiling brightly at him. "And thanks, Kumar. Thanks for everything."

"Oh and by the way," Kumar added. "I won't be at the gas bar this evening at dinner time, so I've put some extra provisions in the bag for you. You must be certain to come and see me here tomorrow morning. And don't forget!"

Sydney tried to put her arm around Turk again as they walked out the door, but he pushed her away. It made Kumar sigh with sadness to see that, and he kept his eyes on them till they disappeared past the parking lot. Kumar prayed that he wasn't making a dreadful mistake.

Turk was in even less of a mood for talking than usual, so the long hike to the Rat River Golf and Country Club was painfully quiet. Sydney tried to start up conversations on a wide range of subjects—whether or not Kumar's dream vision was real (she believed in such things; hadn't a vision led her to Turk in that tree yesterday?), what the inside of the Buick's house was like, what made people like Morton so mean, the best spots to find lost golf balls on the course. She even asked Turk to name his ultimate dream car. But in response to all of that, the only thing Turk said was, "A green convertible 1968 Camaro," which sounded more like their dad's ultimate dream car than Turk's. So the conversation was pretty much one-sided. It wasn't until Sydney asked what presents they should get for Uncle Frank and Aunt Lily that Turk finally spoke up.

"What do you care? You never even cared about finding them anyway. You're just mad at Dad and so you wanted us to run away to teach him a lesson. And now I'm mad at you, so I guess that means I should run away from you too, right?" Turk said, with a face as hard as stone.

Sydney stepped in front of Turk and stopped him right there. She was completely shaken by what he had said, and for a few moments she was too overcome to even speak.

"Don't you dare ever try to run away from me, Turk. Don't ever even say that. Please. Not ever. I am completely sorry about everything, and I'll make it all up to you, I swear. From now on everything's going to be way more fun and a lot more easy. Don't you see it? We could actually live like this and even survive on our own here. But okay—we will phone Dad. I promise."

"When?" Turk asked.

Sydney looked into Turk's brooding face and thought about what to say. Then, for no real reason, the words just popped out. "The day after tomorrow."

Turk put out his hand. Sydney took it and they did their secret handshake—two snaps, two slaps, and one long palm slide. With that, the deal was sealed. Turk remained quiet for the rest of the walk, although he was in a somewhat better mood now, having been reassured by Sydney's promise.

They were at the golf club right on time to meet the Buicks. Again the Buicks were golfing with Mr. and Mrs. Crabstock, and again they were wearing their weirdly permanent smiles. Seeing Bob and Barb Buick gave Turk a queasy feeling. He was sure they'd be able to tell, just by looking at him, that he'd been in their game room yesterday, eating pizza dogs with Brad and Chad. Maybe they'd even know all about what had happened afterwards. Of course, Bob and Barb Buick didn't have the faintest clue. But you can get the sense that if you know all about someone, they must know all about you, too. So Turk kept his distance and tried to disguise himself as a golf bag.

Sydney greeted the Buicks politely and went straight to work, fetching their clubs from the car. Turk scooted after her to help.

"Stay with us in the rough, okay?" Sydney said to him in the parking lot. "I'll be watching for you so don't you try to run away, 'cause, swear to god, I will chase after you. You've got our lunch."

"Only if you give me at least one free golf ball," Turk said.

"Deal," Sydney said, and then they left the parking lot with the clubs.

As the Buicks and Crabstocks headed out to the course with their caddies trailing behind, Turk and Chip stood together outside the pro shop and saw them off. It was like watching a group of explorers heading out on safari.

"Hey. I almost forgot. I got something for you, bud," Chip said. He stepped into the pro shop and returned with an old putter.

"This is from back when I was on the professional golf circuit. I never use it anymore, so you can have it. It'll be good for finding golf balls. Might even find you some luck. It sure did for me. For a while anyway."

"Gee, thanks, Chip," Turk said, taking the putter. It was old and made of wood, and Turk loved the weight of it in his hands. "This is great. Wow, thanks a lot."

"Better get out there, Dusty. There's gold in them there hills," Chip said.

Turk shook Chip's hand and set off toward the golf course.

Everything went smoothly for Sydney that morning. She knew just what to do. The job was simple and she'd easily figured it out the day before, so now she could start to think about other things. Like the Buicks. She'd never met anyone quite like them before. The more she observed them, the more they seemed like characters in a TV show. Or maybe more like actors in a commercial. They smelled nice, even from a distance, and they laughed uproariously at everything, even when nothing was funny. Everything they did and said seemed like it came from a script. Bob Buick had this deep, dark-coffee voice that made his every word sound important yet fake, like a guy on the radio. Sydney wondered how she'd ever be able to ask him about Uncle Frank and Aunt Lily. It would be like talking to a TV screen.

There was someone else that Sydney had started to notice, too. By now she recognized most of the other caddies at the club. To her, they all they seemed sort of goofy and boring—all acting and talking the same dumb way. But there was this one boy named Rene whom Sydney couldn't help noticing, probably because he was so different from the other caddies. While they acted all cocky and carefree,

Rene was shy and quiet. Sydney liked the serious and attentive way he went about his job. He was slim and athletic, with dark skin made even darker from working in the sun. What intrigued her most about him though were his sad black eyes. Why did Rene always look so sad? There was something about his melancholic manner that made Sydney want to know all about him. He was like a mystery to her. And she wanted to see him crack a smile, just once. But he never did. Then, just when she was wondering what made Rene so sad, he glanced in her direction and caught her looking at him. Embarrassed, Sydney quickly looked away.

While the group made the rounds of the golf course, Turk toiled along nearby, searching the rough for balls. No one except Sydney noticed that he was always trailing behind them like a stray dog. He was using the putter that Chip had given him to poke around in the grass and shrubs. That putter worked like magic. By the fifth hole, Turk had already found six balls. For Sydney, it became like a game to try and spot Turk. She would lose sight of him for a while, and then just when she was starting to get anxious, she'd catch a glimpse of him lurking in the trees.

On the eighth hole Bob Buick hooked his drive deep into the rough and Sydney ran in to search for it. She was just picking up the ball when Turk bounced out from behind a tree.

"Boo!" he shouted, and succeeded in giving her a good scare.

"Holy moly! You got me that time, for real," Sydney admitted. "Hey," she said, tossing Bob Buick's golf ball to him, "look what you just found. How many you got so far?"

"This one makes eight. Check this out! Chip gave it to me," Turk said, showing Sydney the antique putter.

"Sweet," Sydney said.

"It's like it has special powers or something. It leads me straight to the balls. I don't even have to try," Turk said.

"Cool," Sydney said.

"So, did you ask him yet?" Turk asked.

"Ask who what yet?"

"Heck, Sydney," Turk said in frustration. "You know? Ask him? Bob Buick? About Uncle Frank and Aunt Lily? Come on, girl, wake up already."

Sydney emerged from the rough and rejoined the golfers on the fairway. "Sorry, Mr. Buick. I couldn't find the darn thing."

"It must have grown legs and run away," Mr. Crabstock said. Bob and Barb Buick cracked up laughing like it was the funniest thing they'd ever heard.

"That's hilarious," Sydney said with her best pretend laugh, trying to join in the fun. She decided that it was time to stop wondering about Rene, and time to start talking to Bob Buick. But Bob Buick only chuckled to himself and told her to go fetch a new golf ball and his number three wood.

How was she ever going to get a chance to ask him about the farm? It's not like she could just blurt out the question. It would seem too weird. She tried to stay close to Bob as he walked down the fairway, waiting for a chance to talk to him. But as far as he was concerned, Sydney was invisible. She was just a caddy. All he cared about was working his sales pitch to Mr. and Mrs. Crabstock.

"I'll tell ya, I think you're really going to love this place," Bob was saying to Mr. Crabstock in his husky salesman voice as they walked down the fairway. "And you know what they say, don't you Jerry? You live like a king in The Royal Woods."

"Well, we'll have a look, Bob, but we've got some doubts. For one thing, that street—what's it called?" asked Mr. Crabstock.

"The street? Fabulous Court Jester Way," Bob said grandly.

"Yeah, well, whatever. Isn't it a little bit out in the sticks?"

"Yes, indeed it is. If by out in the sticks you mean its lovely and tranquil rural setting. So true enough, Jerry, the location is exclusive and private, not to mention highly desirable."

"And way too far from everything," Mr. Crabstock said.

"A mere five minutes' drive from the luxurious Royal Mall, Jerry. And since you'll be our first resident on Court Jester Way, we'll make available that choice corner lot at no additional cost. Just think, Jerry! You will occupy the biggest and most impressive property in the neighbourhood. Imagine how proud your wife and children will be, knowing that your yard is the pride and envy of the entire block. Jerry, you'll truly be a king among peasants."

As soon as Sydney heard Bob mention Court Jester Way, she'd wedged herself right in between the two men as they walked, trying to pick up every word of their conversation. When she heard Bob describing the corner lot, Sydney knew exactly which house they were talking about—the very one that she and Turk were living in.

"Why not bring the wife and kids around this afternoon, Jerry," Bob continued. "Get a feel for the place, and I'm sure that—"

Suddenly, Bob became uncomfortably aware of Sydney's head poking out between he and Mr. Crabstock. "Step back a bit there kid, would ya? When I need your help I'll let you know. Thanks a million," he said in his smooth plummy voice, smiling the whole time.

"Sorry," Sydney said, slowing her pace a bit to let the two men walk ahead, but still trying to stay within earshot.

The first chance she got, Sydney told Turk what she'd just heard. They were on the gravel path through the trees between the thirteenth green and the fourteenth tee, and Sydney had strayed a little bit behind the group, hoping to meet up with Turk.

Sure enough, Turk's head popped out from behind some bushes. "Pssssssst. Hey, Sydney. Did you find out anything?"

"Yeah, I did. Guess what? Bob Buick's gonna sell our house. He's taking Mr. and Mrs. Crabstock there this afternoon, like today. We've got to get back there and get our stuff out."

Sydney had considered sending Turk on ahead, but in light of what had happened yesterday, she decided against it. They would have to run back there together as soon as she finished caddying. It would be disastrous if they couldn't get there in time to retrieve their sleeping bags and clothes. They'd end up losing everything, and replacing it would be difficult and expensive. What was worse, Sydney had stashed most of their money in the house.

When the game was finally over, Turk helped Sydney load the Buick's clubs into their car. "They're having lunch here before they go look at the house," Sydney said. "That'll give us just enough time to get back and grab our stuff. C'mon!"

But there was one thing that Sydney had forgotten about—she was scheduled to caddy for Dr. Gamble later that afternoon.

"Better have your lunch now, Rusty," Chip advised her when they returned to the pro shop to drop off the car keys. "Old Doc Gamble and his party of sawbones will be here in about fifteen minutes."

"I am so sorry, Chip, but I can't," Sydney said anxiously.

"What? Why not?" Chip asked.

"Something's come up. Dusty's not well. I've got to take him to the hospital," she explained.

Chip looked at Turk with concern. He put his hand on his forehead to feel his temperature.

"Seems okay to me," Chip said. "What's the problem, bud?"

"Look," Sydney said, "his thumb's come loose. I think it's going to fall right off."

Turk was double-jointed and could stretch his thumb all the way back to his wrist. It was an old trick, but it never failed to sicken anyone who saw it for the first time. Sydney grabbed his arm, and Turk reluctantly pulled his thumb out of joint and bent it almost to his elbow.

"Ouch!" Chip said. "Yeah, you better get that checked out. How'd you manage that, Dusty?"

"He fell out of a tree into the river yesterday," Sydney explained. "But it didn't start to bug him till just now."

"Fell out of a tree into the river?" Chip asked in horror. "Geez, that's no fun. Listen, there's all kinds of doctors around here. I'll go find a thumb doctor to have a look."

"No," Sydney said with sudden tears welling in her eyes. "I want to get him to the hospital right away!"

Among Sydney's many talents was the ability to cry at will. When Chip saw her tears, he reacted the same way everyone else did whenever she used this trick: he let her do whatever she wanted.

"At least let me drive you there," Chip said, eager to help out anyway he could.

"No, it's okay. We'll get our dad to pick us up," Sydney said, wiping the tears away.

"Well, whatever you say, Rusty. You better get going. Now if only I could find someone to caddy for old Doc Gamble . . ."

"I'll do it," Rene said. He'd been hovering nearby and had overheard their conversation. He looked at Sydney with a funny expression on his face. It wasn't quite a smile, but it was close. It was obvious that Rene knew they were pulling a scam on Chip Long.

"Thanks Rene!" Sydney said. "Thanks Chip! See you tomorrow!"

And then they took off running for the trail. It was too far to run at full speed the whole way, so they paced themselves at a steady jog and soon came to Shep's place. There, a sorry sight greeted them. Someone had demolished Shep's house and smashed up all of his things. Bits and pieces of his house were strewn all over the place, as though a twister had ripped through the clearing. Some of it had even been tossed into the river. They saw his big framed painting of the dogs playing cards floating in the muddy water, and there was his car door sinking just beneath the surface. It was obvious to both of them who had done this.

"Oh, I am so going to fix that guy's wagon," Sydney said with a grim determination in her voice.

There was no time to do anything about it now though. They carried on running the rest of the way to the house, where they flew upstairs and hurriedly packed their stuff. They brought everything down to the kitchen, and were just deciding what to do about the set of doll plates, Halloween decorations, and other weird odds and ends that Shep had given them, when Sydney said, "Wait a minute. I hid our money in the upstairs bathroom. Let me go get it."

She turned to go upstairs just as the front door opened and in walked Bob Buick with the Crabstock family. Sydney ducked back into the kitchen.

"It's all yours folks. Take your time. I'll just wait out in the car while you have a look around," they heard Bob Buick saying. "Jerry, Doris, as I'm sure you know by now, Bob Buick is not some kind of a high-pressure salesman.

That's just not his style. All I want is for you to relax and enjoy this luxurious and stately abode. But folks, I have to tell you—I can feel it. All of you, the whole beautiful Crabstock family, you have truly come home. So welcome home, friends. Welcome to The Royal Woods."

And then Bob Buick gently clicked the door shut and left Jerry and Doris Crabstock and their two kids alone to inspect the house.

Sydney and Turk stared at each other with wide eyes and open mouths. There was no time for them to escape out the back door now. It was Turk who made the first move. He snatched up his backpack from the kitchen floor and slipped down the basement stairs. Sydney quickly followed suit. Once in the basement, they ducked behind the furnace and crouched there, listening to the Crabstock family moving around the house above them.

Even though it was nerve-wracking to be hiding down there, it was also kind of funny. Or at least Sydney thought it was. Turk certainly didn't. For the second day in a row, Turk found himself forced to hide, and it didn't seem any more funny than it had the day before. He wasn't surprised that Sydney was enjoying herself though. Far from being panicked or scared, Sydney's whole being was thrilled with excitement, and she could barely keep herself from busting up laughing.

They could hear every word and sound from upstairs through the air ducts leading from the furnace. Jerry and Doris were bickering away while their two bratty little kids were rampaging around the house, screaming and yelling.

Sydney had to cover her mouth with both hands to choke back her laughter.

"Honey, I just don't know about this master bedroom," Doris whined. "There really isn't adequate closet space, is there?"

"Are you insane?" Jerry replied. "You could park a car in that closet."

While they were debating about the closet space, their two kids were wrestling around in the bedroom that Turk had stayed in. They were so close to an air vent that Sydney and Turk could actually hear them breathing. That's when Sydney got a terrible, evil idea.

She cupped her hands around her mouth and made a low ghost-like moan directly into a vent.

"Whhhoooooooooooo . . ."

The kids kept right on wrestling, so she did it again, louder and longer this time.

"WHHHHHHHHOOOOOooooooooooooooooooooooooooo oooo!"

"What's that!?" they heard one of the kids say.

"Gotcha!" The other kid must have jumped him and pinned him to the floor.

"No! Stop! Shut up for a second," the first kid said.

Sydney moaned into the vent again. "Whhhhhooooooo oooooooooooooo!"

"What is THAT?" the kids cried together in utter terror.

Sydney made her voice sound like a ghost in a horror movie. *"I am the ghost of the vanishing farmer! You must leave this place at once! WHHHHHHHOOOOOOOOOOOOOOOOOOO!"*

The kids' shrill scream was so loud that it even shocked Sydney. The two kids went crashing out into the hallway where they met with their parents, who'd come running to find out what was the matter.

"There's a ghost in the house, Mommy!" one of the kids sobbed. "It was talking to us in the bedroom!"

"I want to go home!" the other kid bawled.

"What is wrong with you two?" Jerry Crabstock scolded. "There are no ghosts. This house is brand new. And you'd better learn to like it, because we're moving in here."

"NO! Daddy! Please! NO!" the two kids howled in unison.

Doris decided to go into the bedroom to investigate, leaving Jerry in the hall scolding the two children. When Doris was alone in the bedroom, Sydney moaned into the duct again.

"WHOOOOOOOOOOOOO. *I am the ghost of the vanishing farmer! Go away! Go away!* Whooooooooooohhhhhhhhhhhh hhhhhhhhhhhh!"

Doris yelped and bolted from the bedroom.

"Honey!" she cried. "There really is something in there! I heard it! It's a poltergeist farmer!"

"Don't be ridiculous," Jerry said angrily. "You're as bad as the kids. It's just the wind or something. Look, I'll go in and check it out and you go down and inspect the kitchen. You guys are starting to drive me nuts."

Whatever was making that sound, Doris Crabstock knew it wasn't the wind. She had a powerful sense that there was some kind of a presence in the house. (And as you know, she was right about that.) With her two trembling children clinging to her sides, she cautiously made her way downstairs and into the kitchen. On seeing the cracked up set of doll plates and cups, the soggy Halloween decorations, and assorted other weird items piled on the kitchen counter, Doris turned white with shock. She tried to scream for her husband, but could only gasp for air.

It was a pure fluke that Shep McParlain Jr. chose that very moment to drop by and visit Sydney and Turk. It was also a pure fluke that he just happened to be wearing a straw farmer's hat and carrying a chicken.

For the previous couple of days, Shep had been rambling along the bank of the Rat River through the farm country south of The Royal Woods. That's the kind of thing Shep would do from time to time. He was prone to forgetting where he lived and the people he knew, and drifting off by himself. Sometimes he'd completely disappear from his former life and start a new life elsewhere. Other times, he'd suddenly remember where he'd come from and head back. You just never knew.

This time, something made Shep remember. Specifically, he remembered Sydney and Turk. When that happened he marched straight back to The Royal Woods to pay them a visit. Along the way, he'd found a chicken that must have escaped from a farm. Further on, he found a straw hat with a hole in it.

You can probably picture the mayhem caused by Shep's sudden appearance, just at the very moment when Doris and her kids were standing there frozen in terror, certain that the house was haunted. With the chicken under his arm and the straw hat on his head, Shep barged in through the back door and burst into the kitchen.

"Kids!" he bellowed. "I'm home!"

Doris Crabstock screamed. The two little kids screamed. Shep screamed. Even the chicken screamed. Then they all stopped screaming to catch their breath. Then they all started screaming again.

When Jerry Crabstock flew down the stairs to find out what all the screaming was about, he almost got run over by his wife and children as they stampeded out the front door. Then he caught a glimpse of Shep and his chicken lurking about inside the kitchen. So there really was a farmer ghost!

"Nice day if it don't rain," Shep said, trying to make conversation.

Jerry gasped in horror and then turned and sprinted straight out of the house after his family. Doris was still screaming as she stuffed the kids into the car. Bob, who'd been lingering around outside waiting for them, watched in disbelief as the entire Crabstock family fled the house in terror and jumped into their car. He hastened over to find out what was wrong, but by then they'd already slammed and locked the car doors.

"Wait! Not enough closet space for you?" Bob shouted at the car. "Don't like the colour scheme? We can redecorate if you—"

Jerry peeled away with his tires squealing, and Bob leapt into his car and chased after them, desperate to make the sale.

When all the commotion was over, and the house went quiet, Sydney and Turk snuck upstairs to investigate what had happened. Both of them thought they'd heard Shep's voice amidst all that noise, but they weren't certain. They peeked around the corner and sure enough, there was Shep McParlain.

"Look who I brought over for a visit," Shep said, proudly holding up the chicken. "Her name's Janet."

CHAPTER ELEVEN

TOO MUCH FUN AT THE FAMILY FUN FAIR

I f you lived in The Royal Woods and happened to look out your window that afternoon, you'd have been treated to a rare sight. It's rare enough to even see anyone out walking in The Royal Woods. Most everyone there is either in a house or in a car. But it would be even rarer still to see three people quite like Sydney, Turk, and Shep go walking past your house, led by a chicken named Janet.

It's worth describing how that looked, just to imagine what someone in The Royal Woods might have thought, had they happened to glance out their window that afternoon. They would have seen a boy of about eight and a girl of about twelve. The boy was wiry and quick on his feet, with dirty blonde hair under a navy blue golf cap, and he carried a backpack, a sleeping bag, and an antique golf putter. He was a sweet-faced boy, with a shy, almost anxious expression. The girl had a ponytail of flaming red hair, and she too was wearing a golf cap and carrying a backpack and a sleeping bag. She was tall for her age, with square shoulders and lanky limbs, and her sharp green eyes took on the world with a sense of keen anticipation and ready confidence.

Aside from the fact that they were carrying backpacks and sleeping bags, there wasn't anything especially unusual about either of the two children. If you saw them pass by your window, you might not have paid them much mind. However, if the chicken they were following didn't get your attention, the man they were walking with most certainly would have. First you might have noticed the man's long, orange beard and the gaping hole in his straw hat. Then you'd see that he was wearing five different coloured shirts under a canary yellow tuxedo jacket. And if you looked closely, you'd notice other things about him as well: the one blue cowboy boot and one red running shoe on his feet, the giant alarm clock tied to a bicycle chain around his neck, and the white satin gloves on his hands. And you'd wonder how he could manage to walk, straight as string, while balancing a tottering tower of pots and pans, Halloween decorations, and doll house plates and cups, all topped by a part from a washing machine. But probably, what you'd wonder most of all is, why?

In fact, Sydney herself had a question for Shep as they walked through The Royal Woods that afternoon.

"So Shep, what's with the shin pads and safety goggles?" she asked, in reference to the pair of kid's silver hockey shin pads he had taped to his legs, and the cracked blue safety glasses that sat lopsided on his face.

"I had a little disagreement with some crows," Shep explained, "and those guys fight dirty. They go straight for the eyes and shins. It's not called a murder of crows for nothing, you know."

It was fun to be talking with Shep again. There hadn't been much time for talk back at the house. Knowing that Bob Buick would soon be back to investigate the scene of the crime, they'd been in a rush to get out of there. After a brief but joyous reunion with Shep, they'd cleaned up everything as best they could, and then spent several frenzied minutes chasing Janet around the house. She seemed to take an immediate liking to the place, and wanted to stay and party. They tried in vain to corner her as she scurried from one room to the next, until Shep finally lost his patience and gave her a scolding. Not with words, but with whistles. He could actually control Janet by whistling. He whistled for her to stop running around like a chicken and do as she was told. Janet obeyed immediately. It was like watching a well-trained dog responding to its master. At Shep's whistling command, Janet emerged from the bathroom and marched straight down the stairs and out the back door. They quickly gathered up all their things and followed her out.

Together they made their way to the Rat River. And so, anyone lucky enough to be looking out their window in

The Royal Woods that afternoon would have been treated to the scene described above.

"Shouldn't we tell him about his house?" Turk whispered to Sydney.

Sydney winced. In all the excitement, she'd forgotten that Shep's house had been destroyed.

"So, Shep," she began hesitantly, "been back by your house lately?"

"What house?" Shep asked.

"You know? Your house. The one by the river? With the car door and stuff."

Shep tilted his head and squinted with a puzzled expression. Then he remembered. "Oh! That house. I forgot all about that place. Nope. Last thing I remember about that place is getting clocked in the head by a golf ball. I never been back since."

"Well," Sydney said sadly, "I'm sorry to say, but we've got some really bad news for you. Someone came along and wrecked it."

"Preposterous," Shep said. "You can't wreck a house like that. You can only rearrange it. See, that's the beauty of your custom-built home. It's way beyond destructible."

Sydney and Turk might have known that they would be more upset about his house than Shep was. He didn't care about possessions in the way most people do. Things were just things to him, and they could be lost or found, destroyed or built, forgotten or remembered—it was all the same to Shep. Even though he felt compelled to collect everything he'd ever found, and loved each and every object he'd ever collected, he never had a sense of ownership over any of it. Shep tramped through life with few cares, unburdened by all the worry about getting and keeping things that seem to weigh so heavily on the rest of us. The world was Shep's junkyard, and his home was inside of him.

※

There was some unusual activity going on at The Royal Shopping Mall that afternoon. As they passed through the back parking lot on their way to the river trail, Sydney, Turk, Shep, and Janet caught a glimpse of a carnival being set up in front of the mall. A crew of workers was busily assembling rides and booths for games of chance on the midway. A huge banner read, "WELCOME TO THE ROYAL WOODS FAMILY FUN FAIR—COME ONE, COME ALL! Brought to you by The Royal Woods Love, Friendship, and Improvement Committee." At the centre of the midway, a gigantic hot-air balloon loomed up behind the banner. It was bright red with broad white stripes, and it stood out razor-sharp against the background of clear blue sky. The balloon's most striking feature was the likenesses of Mr. and Mrs. Buick printed on its sides—Barb on one side and Bob on the other. Their big smiling faces bobbed and swayed in the breeze, gazing over The Royal Woods like giant happy zombies.

"Cool!" Turk exclaimed. "Sydney! Can we go there?"

"Sure," Sydney said. "Why not? First let's help Shep out though. And we've still got to figure out where we're going to stay now."

"Heck. I forgot about that," Turk said. "Where are we going to stay anyway?"

"Still got that little screwdriver, Shep?" Sydney asked.

"You read my mind Syd," Shep grinned.

Shep led the way down the trail, somehow managing to balance that impossible stack of plates and things in his hands, even over rough ground, whistling all the while.

"You know Shep," Sydney observed, "you really should be a circus act."

"Been there done that, Syd," Shep sighed. "Long story and I won't go into it now, but I will give you a word of advice: never trust a clown."

When they got to the clearing, Shep immediately set to work rebuilding his house. He was right. A house like that really couldn't be destroyed. Even though much of it had been smashed or tossed into the river, there were still plenty of usable things lying around. It didn't matter to Shep if they were broken or not—he found a use for everything. What most impressed Sydney and Turk was the pleasure Shep took in his work. Whistling and singing, Shep rolled up his sleeves (all five of them on each arm) and went at the job with gusto. It was hard not to believe that Shep was actually glad someone had wrecked his house. The task of rebuilding it provided a focus for his relentless energy. Sydney and Turk tried to help, but Shep was so quick and skilful, there wasn't much for them to do except gather up the bits and pieces they found strewn around the clearing, and stack them into a neat pile for Shep to use as he saw fit.

Before long, the house was as good as ever. In fact, it

was better than ever, or at least that's what Sydney and Turk thought. Since it had been built with fewer things this time, the house was simpler and less cluttered than before. That's not how Shep saw it though.

"Well, it's a start I guess," Shep said, gravely inspecting the new structure with hands on hips. "Still a long way to go on the project, but it's a start."

"Lunchtime!" Sydney sang.

Kumar had packed a ton of food for them. There were chapattis, boiled eggs, carrot sticks, samosas, pakoras, oranges and apples, mango juice, and for dessert, Shep's favourite—Hawaiian doughnuts.

After they'd finished eating, Sydney and Turk felt too lazy to do anything except hang around the clearing for the rest of the day. Finding another house to stay in could wait until dark. So could the family fun fair at the mall. It was a blistering hot afternoon, and it was nice to be able to just relax in the cool shade and take a break from everything for a change. Finding themselves with Shep again came as a most welcome surprise—they'd long since thought they'd seen the last of him. Hanging around at Shep's place seemed like the easiest and most pleasant thing to do in the whole world. It felt so comforting and familiar, especially for Turk. Knowing that their old ally Shep was back made him less anxious about going home or phoning their dad.

Sydney had a nap under a tree, Turk played with Janet by the river (she could swim!), and Shep continued renovations on his house. And in that way the drowsy afternoon drifted by. It wasn't until the mosquitoes started to take over the Rat River for the evening that Sydney and Turk felt inclined to make a move.

The first thing they needed to deal with was getting another house to stay in.

"I say we get another one on Court Jester Way," Sydney said. "After all, it's the only street we like in the whole entire neighbourhood."

On their way past the mall, they saw that the family fun fair was in full swing. The lights of the midway dazzled brightly in the early evening dusk, the smell of hotdogs filled the air, and the sound of kids whooping it up mingled with the music and roar of the rides. It all looked so inviting to Turk, he could hardly wait to go.

But first they had to find a new house. This turned out to be as easy as pie. With the help of Shep and his trusty little screwdriver, Sydney and Turk moved into a house identical to their first one, just three doors away. They unpacked their things and rolled out their sleeping bags in bedrooms that were exactly the same as the ones they'd slept in for the previous three nights. It felt like they'd never left.

After they'd gotten themselves all sorted out in their new house, Sydney would have been content to stay in for the night. She had a big day of caddying ahead of her, and she could have used a good night's sleep. But they needed something to eat, and for sure nothing was going to stop Turk from checking out the fun fair. And so, unfortunately, off they all went.

It was unfortunate because the fun fair turned out to be the start of some serious trouble for Sydney and Turk. Of course, as you know, they'd had trouble before in The Royal Woods—plenty of trouble. But this was to be the start of their most serious trouble yet.

Sydney and Turk probably should have realized that bringing Shep and his pet chicken Janet to a family fun fair at a brand new suburban subdivision shopping mall was just asking for trouble. But by then, Sydney and Turk had become so accustomed to Shep and his ways that it hardly occurred to them how strange and even frightening he was to other people. Especially women and children. To put it mildly, their arrival at The Royal Woods Family Fun Fair caused a stir.

The crowd cleared a path for them as they walked down the midway. Everyone stopped and stared. Some pointed and snickered, while others gazed in stunned silence. Small children whimpered and hid behind their mothers. Teenage boys jeered and laughed. Fathers studied them warily, as though the very presence of this odd little group threatened to steal all the fun from the family fun fair.

"We better stick together," Sydney cautioned. "This could turn ugly."

Oblivious to all the fuss he was causing, Shep ambled along the midway whistling sweet tropical bird songs, while Janet sat perched on his shoulder clucking with excitement. Sydney hadn't been keen on coming in the first place, but when she saw the hostile reception they were getting, she naturally became determined to stay and enjoy herself. She'd brought exactly twenty-five dollars of her hard-earned caddying money for them to spend on food and amusements, and she planned to spend every penny. After all, they had as much right to have fun at the family fun fair as anyone.

It was all a bit too much for Turk though.

"Maybe we should come back tomorrow," he said uneasily.

"Why should we?" Sydney shrugged. "Let's have some fun."

They bought hotdogs and pop and found a picnic table to sit down on. "So what do you guys want to do first?" Sydney asked brightly, pretending not to notice the discomforted glares of the people eating nearby.

"Well, since you asked," Shep said, "I'd like to try out some of those feats of strength and skill-testing games. And for sure Janet wants a pony ride."

"Okay, cool. What about you Turk?"

"I just want one ride on the Cosmic Frog and maybe also to try out the Face Ripper," Turk said.

"Let's do the rides first and then check out the games," Sydney suggested.

It was while Turk was riding the Cosmic Frog that all the trouble started. Sydney and Shep were standing on the ground watching Turk being hurtled around above them in a spinning green frog car when three members of The Royal Woods Love, Friendship and Improvement Committee walked over and asked them to leave the family fun fair.

There were two men and one woman, and you could tell they were committee members because they all wore matching purple hats and purple T-shirts that said, "Kiss me! I'm Royalty!" in fancy gold letters.

"What's the problem?" Sydney asked. "We're not hurting anyone, are we?"

"The problem is, young lady, live poultry is not allowed at the family fun fair," said the woman. She was a tiny woman with a twitchy tanned frown, and she stood toe to toe and face to face with Sydney, while the two men looming behind her looked on sourly. The name tag on the woman's T-shirt said, "Dee Dee—Family Fun Fair Chairperson."

"Wait a minute. You mean to tell me there's rules about chickens at family fun fairs?" Sydney asked in disbelief. "Since when?"

"Since now," Dee Dee said. "We don't want any trouble, so please just leave the family fun fair quietly."

"I don't think so," Sydney replied coolly. "Not until we've had some fun. We just got to the family fun fair, and I have to tell you honestly, Dee Dee, so far? We haven't had any fun at all."

"Aren't you the cheeky little thing," the women bristled, which was sort of funny considering she was the exact same height as Sydney. Dee Dee turned to the two men at her side, "Fritz, Dieter, would you please escort these people and their chicken out of the family fun fair?"

One of the men reached out to take Sydney by the arm, but she jerked away. "Don't even think about it, Fritz."

The ride had finished by then and Turk walked over to join them.

"What's going on?" he asked.

"Hey, Turk, these nice people from The Royal Woods Love, Friendship and Improvement Committee are welcoming us to the family fun fair. They want to show us around," Sydney explained.

"Really?" Turk asked.

"Yeah," Sydney said. "So what's next, folks? How about some of those fun games?"

Shep, who had been staring off into space throughout the entire conversation, suddenly tuned in when he heard the word "game" mentioned. "Let's get at 'er," he said, rubbing his hands in eager anticipation. "Daddy needs a brand new plush toy."

With the three committee members following right at their heels, they walked down the midway checking out the games. It looked like they were being flanked by their own personal, purple uniformed body guards. If they hadn't been already, by now they were most certainly the centre of attention at the fair.

"Sydney," Turk said, "what the heck?"

"This is so cool," Sydney beamed. "I feel like a celebrity," she said, waving and twirling around once. "I'd like to thank the Academy and all my fans for believing in me!"

The first game to catch Shep's attention was the Dirt Toss of the Ancient Pharaohs, in which you were challenged to fling a spoonful of dirt into a milk bottle about twenty feet away. Shep wandered over and waited in line to play.

A bored-looking man wearing a fake beard and an Egyptian robe sat on a stool in the booth, droning into a microphone: "Toss the dirt and have some fun, everyone's a winner, test your skills at the ancient art of tossing dirt into a bottle, step right up folks, win a prize just for tossing dirt, relive the lifestyle of the ancient pharaohs, fun for the entire family, memories to last a lifetime, you'll laugh you'll cry but you'll never wonder why, when you're tossing dirt with a spoon, so step right up . . ." And so on.

It looked to be an impossible task. They watched as one contestant after another flung spoonfuls of dirt into the air, only to groan in frustration as the dirt clots fell miserably short of the milk bottle. Next it was Shep's turn. He spit into his gloved hands and rubbed them together, picked up a spoonful of dirt and readied himself. He wiggled his hips, closed one eye, and with a tiny flick of the wrist, sent the clot of dirt sailing through the air and straight into the milk bottle.

Sydney and Turk cheered wildly and there were high-fives all around. The committee members stood grimly glowering with their arms folded as Shep collected his prize.

"Congratulations, boss," the man in the booth muttered, "have a shark. Now hit the road." He handed Shep a plush blue shark that was twice as big as Turk.

"Are we having fun yet, young lady?" Dee Dee asked.

"We're getting there, thanks," Sydney said. "Now, how about a ride on that Face Ripper?"

"Yeah!" Turk enthused.

On the Face Ripper, you lie down inside a long glass tube with your head sticking out the front. Then you're raised up in the air and spun around and around so fast that it feels just like your face is being ripped right off your head. Turk enjoyed it so much that he rode it twice. Sydney and Shep stayed on the ground smiling up at him, while the three committee members stood nearby watching them and not smiling.

"This sure is a fun family fun fair," Sydney said. "But you don't look like you're having any fun at all, Dee Dee. How come?"

"Don't get saucy with me, young lady," she scolded. "Just have your fun and get out of here."

After Turk was finished with his second ride, Shep tried his luck at two more games: Tickle Me Pig, in which you tickle a twenty-pound guinea pig until it laughs out loud, and Push the Tow Truck over the Stump, in which you push a tow truck over a tree stump, obviously. Shep easily won both games, and his prizes included a convincingly lifelike sculpture of the Queen of England's head made out of used chewing gum, and an even more lifelike plush Bengal tiger that was even bigger than the shark he'd won earlier. The tiger looked so real that Janet squawked in terror when Shep wrestled it over his other shoulder.

"Just settle down there, sister. He won't hurt you," Shep said to Janet, which seemed to reassure her.

"We've got enough money for two more games or one more ride," Sydney said. "What do you guys want to do?"

"Let's not forget about that pony ride," Shep said.

You can hardly imagine what Shep looked like just then, standing there so intently in the midway, clutching a giant plush shark and a bust of Queen Elizabeth, with a fake Bengal tiger over one shoulder and a real live chicken perched on the other.

"Oh, yeah!" Sydney giggled. "This I've got to see."

"Wait just a second, young lady," Dee Dee said. "If we let you try the pony ride, do you promise to leave the fun fair immediately after?"

Sydney chewed on her lip and considered the offer. She realized that Dee Dee must be thinking the pony ride was for Turk, not Janet. It would be fun to give the committee members a small surprise before they left the Fun Fair.

"Sure," Sydney said, "We've only got enough money for a pony ride anyways. And before I forget, thanks for taking the time to show us around the family fun fair, Dee Dee, if that is your real name. We've had loads of fun. Maybe we'll come back tomorrow for some more."

Dee Dee's face twisted into a tortured smile. "I don't think so."

There was a small surprise for Sydney herself at the pony ride. Rene, the caddy from the country club, was working there selling tickets.

"Hey," Rene said when he saw Sydney, "how's it going?"

"Good," Sydney said shyly. Suddenly, and for the first time, she found herself somewhat embarrassed at being with Shep. What would Rene think?

"Are you, like, working here?" Sydney asked, not knowing what else to say.

"Well yeah, I guess I must be," Rene said.

To her horror, Sydney felt herself blushing terribly.

"Excuse me there, compadre," Shep said to Rene. "Is it half price for chickens or do they have to pay the full fare?"

"Pardon?" Rene asked.

"You know, for the pony ride," Shep explained.

It was then, also for the first time, that Sydney saw Rene smile. His whole face just lit up with delight. Sydney thought her own face was about to burst into flames from blushing.

"Chickens ride free," Rene laughed, tearing off a ticket for Shep.

The committee members were off to the side, huddled together talking, so they still had no idea what was about to happen. At Shep's whistling instruction, Janet hopped off his shoulder and strutted over to the ponies. She inspected each of them carefully, and then selected a lovely little palomino. With a quick leap and a flap of her wings, Janet landed on the back of the pony.

Then all hell broke loose.

Probably nothing would have happened, and they could have left the fun fair quietly, if the crowd hadn't erupted in outrage at the sight of Janet riding the pony. The problem wasn't with Janet. She appeared to be a skilled and experienced rider, and had no difficulty controlling the little palomino. But what with all the yelling and screaming, the pony began to panic.

"Hey! What's that chicken doing on a pony?" someone in the crowd shouted.

"Yeah! Get that chicken off the pony!" someone else cried out.

"That's just not right!" a woman sobbed.

"Chickens should *not* ride ponies!" another person shouted.

"That chicken's ruining the family fun fair!" bawled another, followed by a blood-curdling scream of anguish.

Faster and faster Janet circled the little track on the pony. Louder and louder the roar of the crowd grew. Responding to the outraged mob, the three committee members leapt into action. They sprinted over and began chasing after Janet as she rode around the track, yelling for her to stop the pony. It was too late though—the pony was out of control and all Janet could do was hold on for dear life.

"Good people of The Royal Woods!" Shep bellowed. "I implore you to remain calm! The chicken means no harm! I repeat—the chicken means no harm!" But it was all in vain. The crowd only became louder and more hysterical. Shep tried to whistle for Janet to stop, but she couldn't possibly hear him over all that noise.

Then Dee Dee made the mistake of trying to stop the pony by jumping in front of it with her hand held up like a traffic cop. Not only was she knocked flying into the big vat beside the cotton candy machine, she so startled the pony that it bolted from the track and took off across the parking lot. The crowd gasped in horror. Everyone stood there in shocked silence and watched as the little pony galloped away toward the open prairie with Janet bouncing wildly in the saddle.

When the chicken and pony completely disappeared from sight, the crowd swung around and faced Sydney, Turk and Shep.

Dee Dee pulled herself out of the sticky vat of cotton candy and pointed straight at Sydney. "Now do you see why chickens are not allowed at the family fun fair, young lady?" Dee Dee wailed. And then she burst into tears.

CHAPTER TWELVE

THE NOTORIOUS THREE

Y ikes," Rene said, "I think you guys better skedaddle on out of here."

That was pretty obvious. When an angry mob of people turns on you and starts booing and throwing things, there isn't much choice about what to do next—you have to flee the scene immediately. And that's just what Sydney, Turk, and Shep did after the first plastic cup sailed in their direction, followed by a bag of popcorn, an ice cream cone, a half-eaten corn dog, a giant pretzel, and even a baby bottle. Having things thrown at him was nothing new for Shep, but Sydney and Turk had never experienced anything like it before. Shocked and humiliated, they skulked out of the fairgrounds with their heads down, while the crowd continued to boo and pelt them with things.

All the way back to Shep's place, Turk was sullen and silent. Sydney was silent, too—at first. But by the time they got to the riverbank, she was fully launched into a bitter tirade about the terrible treatment they'd been given, and how they hadn't done anything to deserve it. Furthermore, she denounced The Royal Woods and all of its inhabitants in the most colourful language she could think of (none of which will be repeated here). "Sydney, please," Turk said. "There's a child present." Of course Shep just whistled away like nothing had happened, although he did mention that he'd have to get up early tomorrow to search for Janet and the runaway pony. Overall, the evening had been a smashing success for Shep, and he had the prizes to prove it.

After walking Shep back to his place, Sydney and Turk returned to their new house for the night. It was strange and a little bit spooky to be back inside that big empty house all by themselves, and they both had a hard time falling asleep. Not wanting to be alone, Turk rolled out his sleeping bag in Sydney's room. They both sensed that the calamity at the fun fair had changed everything for them, although neither of them wanted to talk about it. After all that time living secretly and anonymously, they had suddenly become very well-known in The Royal Woods, even notorious. They tossed and turned in their sleeping bags, both plagued by a nagging sense of dread about what tomorrow might bring. When he finally did fall asleep, Turk had terrible dreams, including one about being chased around the fairgrounds by family fun fair committee members wearing purple T-shirts and riding ponies, while the sky rained golf balls.

Before they left the house the next morning, Sydney decided that it would be a good idea to take their backpacks and sleeping bags with them, just to be on the safe side. She didn't want to risk losing all their stuff if Bob Buick came along to show the house to some potential buyers. What's more, under the circumstances, she wanted to be ready to flee The Royal Woods in an instant if they encountered any trouble.

Trekking through the wide open expanse of The Royal Woods was very unsettling that morning. They felt exposed and obvious when they both wished that they could be invisible. There weren't even any back lanes or short cuts for them to use, so they had to walk right through the centre of the treeless neighbourhood in plain view of everyone. It was still early in the morning, but already it was hot, and the day promised to be a real scorcher—the hottest day yet.

Their unease was made even worse when they arrived at the mall to find that the Family Fun Fair was getting ready to start up for the day. It was weird to see the fairgrounds in the bright light of day. The most disturbing thing of all was the big smiling face of Bob Buick on the side of the hot-air balloon. His grinning eyes seemed to follow them as they scurried across the sprawling parking lot toward the safe harbour of the Chubby Princess Doughnut Cottage. They were desperate to get inside the doughnut shop, and longing for Kumar's warm and happy good morning greeting.

But the doughnut shop was the least safe place for them that morning. An emergency meeting of The Royal Woods Love, Friendship, and Improvement Committee was being held there, and the sole topic of conversation was the crazy bird man, the two wicked children who were tagging around with him, and the disgrace and scandal all three of them were bringing to the entire community. There were angry speeches and calls for swift and decisive action.

From his place behind the counter, Kumar listened in on the meeting with growing alarm. Of course he knew exactly who the committee was discussing. It was awful for Kumar to listen to the terrible things being said about the trio, especially when he heard them describing Sydney and Turk as being a menace to the neighbourhood, and a threat to the safety of their own children.

"We really have no choice, people," Dee Dee cried. "For the sake of our precious children, the trash bird man must be arrested and put in jail for illegal poultry possession and horse theft at the family fun fair. And his two wicked accomplices must be apprehended and sent to an orphanage!"

Her proposal was greeted with a roar of cheers and applause, which made Kumar feel so sick he thought he would have to lie down on the floor and have a nap.

At that very moment, Sydney and Turk were nearing the doughnut shop. Desperate to get inside and see Kumar,

Turk burst ahead and sprinted the last hundred yards across the parking lot. It was a good thing that Kumar was paying close attention to the meeting, and had been anticipating the arrival of Sydney and Turk. When Turk came skipping through the door with a big smile on his face, the first thing he saw was Kumar frantically shaking his head and waving his hands for him to turn back. It took less than a second for Turk to realize that something was horribly wrong. He made a swift about-face and slipped back outside just as Sydney arrived.

"What's up?" Sydney asked.

"I don't know," Turk said, "but it looks serious. There's a big crowd of people yelling about stuff, and Kumar waved at me not to come in."

Sydney crouched down and peeked through the window. Everyone in the jam-packed doughnut shop was wearing purple T-shirts. Bob Buick was standing and addressing the crowd, with his wife Barb seated on one side of him and Dee Dee on the other, both wearing angry frowns. Bob looked angry too, although somehow the tight smile remained fixed on his face.

"What do you think they're talking about?" Turk asked.

"Us, probably. But especially Shep, I bet. We better go warn him," Sydney said. "I don't like the looks of this at all. Come on, let's get the heck out of here."

"Wait a minute," Turk said. "Don't you remember what today is?"

"Uhm, Thursday? Or no, wait. It's Friday. I think," Sydney said.

"It's the day after tomorrow," Turk said.

"What do you mean?"

"What I mean is, it's the day after tomorrow from the day when you said we were going to phone dad. Remember?"

"Is it? Oh yeah, right. I guess it is. But listen, we really can't phone him right now Turk, there's way too much going on. First we have to go warn Shep, and then we have to get to the golf course. I bet I could make, like, over sixty bucks today, and you can find some golf balls and—"

"Sydney," Turk interrupted.

He didn't have to say another word. Sydney had given Turk a sincere promise about that phone call, and there was no way out of it now. Even though she'd made it in a moment of weakness, and had only done so to make Turk content and keep him on her side, a promise is a promise. Still, she was surprised that Turk hadn't forgotten all about it by now, considering everything that had happened since then. Sydney sure had.

Turk had been planning on making the phone call from the doughnut shop, but since that was obviously impossible, he sped across the parking lot toward the pay phone beside the gas bar. Sydney had to run to catch up with him. By the time she got there, Turk was already holding the phone and waiting for her to instruct him on how to make a collect call. Sydney would have also liked to instruct him on what to say to their dad, but she couldn't think of what those instructions should be. Watching Turk make that phone call, Sydney felt powerless, as though this was happening in a book or a movie, and all she could do was wait and see what would happen next.

Have you ever phoned home from a long way away and listened to the sound of the ring? If you close your eyes and listen closely, it's almost like you can see the inside of your house. The ring sounds familiar, and quite unlike the sound of any other phone ringing. Or so it seemed to Turk. As he hung on listening to that ring with his eyes shut tight, Turk could see all the things in his kitchen at home—the chairs and the table beside the ringing phone, the stove and fridge, the sink full of dishes, the calendar on the wall with a picture of a mountain. Then his mind travelled out of the kitchen and into the living room, and he saw everything there too; all the usual clutter and chaos. Turk continued to tour his house, and was heading down the hall toward his bedroom when he suddenly realized it—no one was home. The phone was ringing in an empty house.

Just as that awful realization struck him, the operator came on and said, "No one is answering to accept the charges. Could you please try again later?"

Turk hung up without a word.

Sydney should have felt relieved that their dad wasn't home to answer the phone, but she didn't. How could she feel anything but wretched when she saw the stricken look on her little brother's face as he hung up and stepped out of the phone booth?

"Don't worry, we'll try again later. He must be at work," Sydney said.

"It's Saturday, by the way," Turk said. "Dad doesn't work on Saturday. It's Saturday morning and Dad's supposed to be at home reading the paper and listening to the radio, just like always."

"We'll see," Sydney said. "Next chance we get, we'll try him again. Don't worry, you'll talk to Dad today. For sure. Come on."

They gathered up their things and walked across the parking lot toward the river. Not wanting to embarrass him, Sydney observed Turk out of the corner of her eye, certain that he was about to start crying. But Turk didn't cry. He could have, she knew, and he should have too. It would probably make him feel a little better. But Turk didn't want to cry, and his face had a faraway look, as though he was trying hard to think of something else to keep from crying. Instead, to her surprise, Sydney found that she was the one whose eyes were beginning to fill with tears.

"What's wrong?" Turk asked. "Are you crying?"

"No," Sydney sniffed. "I must be allergic to something here. I think I'm allergic to The Royal Woods."

Luckily, there was a good laugh waiting for them at Shep's place. The Bengal tiger that he'd won at the family fun fair was sprawled across the roof of his shack. It looked so real and alive that they both started in surprise when they first saw it there. The tiger had a note in its mouth which read: "Dear S and T, Gone pony hunting. Left the tiger to guard the house against trespassers. See you for dinner? LOVE, Shep McParlain Jr. P.S: There's bruised turnips and black-eyed Brussels sprouts inside if you're hungry. Help yourselves!"

"I love Shep," Sydney smiled. "That guy just kills me. Here, let's leave our stuff in his house and pick it up later." They threw their backpacks and sleeping bags into the shack and set off for the golf course.

It seemed that they could always rely on Shep to put them in a good mood. That tiger on the roof with the note in its mouth gave them something to talk and laugh about all the way to the golf course, and suddenly everything seemed less serious. The big commotion at the family fun fair was actually quite hilarious, now that they thought about it. And they really hadn't done anything wrong, so there was nothing to fear. After a couple of days, everyone would probably forget the whole thing had ever happened. They'd forget about Sydney and Turk too, and then everything would return to normal. As for today, they'd work hard at the golf course, and then meet up with Shep and take him for dinner at the gas bar with Kumar. And Turk could still make that phone call home anytime he wanted.

In short, it was just another day in The Royal Woods.

***

"The Red Witch," Bob Buick turned and said, right after he'd smacked his ball off the first tee.

"Who?" Mr. Shrub asked.

It was just the two men golfing that morning, with Sydney caddying for Bob Buick and Rene caddying for Mr.

Shrub, a small monkey-faced man who happened to be president of The Royal Woods Love, Friendship and Improvement Committee.

"Her real name's Sydney," Bob explained, "but Dee Dee's son Morton calls her the Red Witch. She's that wild, red-headed kid who hangs around with the trash bird man."

Sydney was blushing three shades of crimson as Bob handed her his driver and she dropped it into the golf bag.

"She's got this warlock little brother, too, and they go rampaging around the neighbourhood with the trash bird man," Bob continued as he strode down the fairway. "Dee Dee told me they almost drowned poor little Morton in the river, and tried to kill him and my twin boys with some poisoned Hawaiian doughnuts. They even snuck into my house and tried to steal our pizza dog supply. But what really gets my dander up is that they've been living in vacant houses in The Royal Woods. They blew a sale for me over on Court Jester Way. The trash bird man showed up and freaked out my clients. And then last night, they came along and stole all the fun from the family fun fair."

"It's an outrage," Mr. Shrub said, shaking his head.

To hear herself, Turk and Shep being talked about in that way gave Sydney a new and queasy sensation. For a moment, it felt like she was floating outside of her own body, watching and listening to Bob talk from somewhere above. It was amazing that Bob hadn't put two and two together and realized that the so-called Red Witch was his very own personal caddy, and that the warlock was her little brother Turk. But thank goodness for that. And thank goodness that Turk hadn't heard a word of this conversation. Just hearing that Dee Dee was Morton's mom might have caused Turk to faint in shock. Luckily, Turk had carefully avoided going anywhere near Bob Buick that morning, and had set off hunting for golf balls the moment they'd arrived at the country club.

"They're a menace, a threat, a scourge, and a scandal. And very bad for business too, I might add," Bob said to Mr. Shrub. "But not for long. As soon as we're done here, the emergency task force subcommittee will show the police where the bird man lives, his shack will be torn down and hauled away, and then all three culprits will be apprehended and removed from The Royal Woods forever. It's time to take out the garbage around here."

Having said that, Bob ripped a seven-iron over the sand and nicely onto the green.

"Nice shot sir," Sydney said, but Bob didn't pay her any attention.

Sydney didn't need to (and in fact couldn't bear to) hear any more. She slowed her pace and let Bob and Mr. Shrub get ahead of her and well out of earshot. Rene slowed down to walk along side her, just to keep her company. The two of them walked together in silence for the next couple of holes. Now for certain, Sydney realized, it was all over for them in The Royal Woods. She and Turk would have to leave immediately. But where could they go? She'd have to think about that very hard and, hopefully, by the time she finished caddying, she'd have a plan.

Rene was the kind of person who was comfortable with silence, and there was nothing for him to say anyway. He didn't know all there was to know about their situation, but he realized that Sydney, her little brother Turk and their friend Shep were in serious trouble. It wasn't his way to pry into other people's business. But Sydney was the talkative sort, with a burning need to share whatever thoughts and feelings she had at any given moment. She'd hoped that Rene might ask her a few questions. When he didn't, she started to volunteer both the questions and the answers herself.

"You know what really bugs me about all this?" she asked Rene when they were walking down the fairway on the fourth hole. "All that land, the whole place where The Royal Woods is now? All those houses, the mall, the school—everything? It all used to be our relatives' farm. It belonged to my dad's aunt and uncle. The Buicks just came along and stole it from them, and now they act like they're the king and queen of the whole place and they can do whatever they want, like chase people off and put them in jail if they don't like them. It's so unfair!"

Rene smiled sadly. "That's nothing new around here. I know all about that kind of thing. I'm Métis."

"What do you mean?" Sydney asked.

"Before The Royal Woods, before that farm, before this golf course, before everything—all of it and more was where the Métis hunted buffalo. You seen many buffaloes around here lately?"

Sydney was embarrassed by her ignorance on the subject. She'd never heard of the Métis, and had never given a thought as to what was there before the farm. It made her eager to find out more—she took a keen interest in everything, and always had to know as much about the world as she could. There were a thousand things she wanted to learn from Rene, but after answering her first twenty questions or so, Rene said, "You should read a book or something. There's way too much to tell."

They were standing beside the green while Bob and Mr. Shrub putted when Rene caught a glimpse of Shep, casually leading the pony with Janet in the saddle across the next fairway. Rene nudged Sydney and tilted his head in Shep's direction. The sight made her burst out laughing. Bob and Mr. Shrub looked around to see what was so funny. Fortunately, neither of the two men spotted Shep, who had slipped into the trees on the riverbank by then.

Sydney turned serious. "I hope I can get back in time to warn Shep. And, oh no," she groaned. "I just remembered. We left all our stuff in his house. What if the cops come and take it all away before we get there?"

Sydney was beginning to have another worry, too. Where was Turk? She'd been checking for him in the rough all morning, but hadn't seen him since the second hole.

Sydney would have been relieved and pleased—if a little bit jealous—to know that at that very moment, Turk was enjoying a sumptuous buffet breakfast at the clubhouse. Breakfast had always been Turk's favourite meal of the day, and that morning he was experiencing the Greatest Breakfast in History. The feast had come about thanks to his old friend, Chip Long.

Turk hadn't lasted long searching for balls that morning. For one thing, he'd forgotten the lucky putter that Chip had given him back at their new house, and so he hadn't managed to find even one golf ball. Plus, in all the excitement that morning, they didn't get a chance to eat anything, so Turk was too hungry to focus on the job. But above all, the one thing on Turk's mind that day was phoning his dad. Now that he knew how to make a collect call, he decided to go to the clubhouse and try again.

Chip saw Turk in the clubhouse just as he'd hung up the phone. Again there'd been no answer, and again Turk didn't cry.

"Hey Dusty, how's it going, bud? You don't look so good. That thumb still bothering you?" Chip asked.

"No. It's all better now, thanks," Turk said.

"Maybe you just need something to eat. It'll be my treat. Come on."

Chip set up Turk at his own special table on the veranda overlooking the golf course, and left instructions with the staff to let the boy eat anything he wanted. Turk took full advantage of the buffet table. He started with the Belgian waffles and whipped cream, moved on to the French toast and maple syrup, and then had a go at the German strudel and ice cream. When he was all finished, Turk felt as though he'd just conquered and eaten most of western Europe. He washed it all down with about a gallon of fresh-squeezed orange juice.

Turk felt much better after he'd eaten. In fact, he was completely content for the moment. If he could have moved, Turk would have gotten up and tried phoning his dad again. But he was too stuffed to move. All he could do was sit relaxing at the table, gazing out at the golf course, and try not to fall asleep from the effects of the big breakfast.

The weather was changing, which made Turk feel even more sleepy. The air was soupy thick and still, and he could feel its weight pressing down on him. Off in the distant horizon, Turk could see a dark wedge in the sky which he first thought must be the smoke from a fire. But it was too big to be smoke, and it wasn't the right colour either. It was the colour of a bruise, so dark purple that it was almost black, and it was advancing slowly and growing ever bigger. Then Turk realized that it was actually a bank of clouds, but quite unlike any clouds he'd ever seen before. The clouds formed a living curtain in the sky, boiling and roiling with colour as they got closer—black and blue, purple and grey, even bottle green and chestnut brown.

Turk was mesmerized by the sight. It was like watching a dream. It was while gazing at those clouds that Turk saw what at first seemed to be part of the dream, but then suddenly turned into something more like a nightmare. There was Bob Buick, followed by his caddy Sydney, walking toward the clubhouse from the eighteenth hole. And there were the twins, Brad and Chad Buick, with their mom Barb, walking out of the clubhouse to meet them. With the dark curtain of clouds forming a backdrop to the scene, it all seemed very much like the end of the world to Turk. Planets were about to collide.

Now Turk really did have to move, and move he did. He sprang out of his chair and leapt over the side of the veranda. It was too late for him to warn Sydney, but he sped toward her anyway. Turk couldn't hear what was being said as the twins and their mom on one side, and Sydney and Bob Buick on the other, all met up together near the caddy shack. As he ran toward them, it was like watching a cartoon on TV with the sound off. Everyone acted out their shock with stunned faces and jerky gestures. Just as Turk had expected, Sydney didn't stick around to try and explain herself. She simply dropped the golf clubs right then and there, and took off running.

"Turk! There you are!" Sydney said with relief when Turk came sprinting up to her side. "Come on! Let's get the heck out of here! We gotta find Shep."

They didn't look back once as they ran out of the country club toward the trail by the river. Once on the trail, it wasn't long before they came upon Shep, whistling and chatting with Janet on the pony as they ambled along. Sydney and Turk took a moment to catch their breath.

"Way to go, Shep. How'd you find them?" Sydney asked.

"I just followed my nose," Shep explained. "You see, the horse and chicken together have a very distinctive scent, especially when they're scared. They were halfway to Hudson's Bay when I finally caught up with them. This pony's going straight home to the family fun fair. And by the way, in case you didn't notice, there's a storm a-brewing."

He was obviously right about that. The sky was still clear blue directly above them, and the sun was burning hotter than ever. But the wedge of clouds in the sky to the northwest was as dark as night and as high as a mountain, and it was headed in their direction, pushed by a blasting wind that whipped the treetops all around them.

"Yeah I know, we better hurry," Sydney said. "Listen Shep, the police are coming to arrest you, and they're going to take me and Turk, too. We've got to get back to your place and get our stuff, drop the pony off at the fair and get the heck out of here. I've got a really great idea. Let's go!"

"Wait a minute," Turk called into the wind, clutching the hat on his head with both hands. "What really great idea? We've had tons of really great ideas lately, and almost none of them turned out to be so great after all. Let's just stop and think about this great idea first."

"Trust me Turk, it's a really great idea. And there's no time for talk now. Come on, let's go!" Sydney said, and with that she took off running toward Shep's place. This was precisely the kind of action and adventure that Shep loved, and he set off eagerly after Sydney, with Janet on the pony galloping along behind him. Turk had no choice but to go with the flow.

They ran down the trail until they came to the rise just above the big bent-over tree by the river. Sydney halted and held up her hands to signal stop. The others caught up and pushed in behind her.

"Well, holy moly," Sydney said. "What have we here?"

Down at the bottom of the rise was Morton, busily carving something into the big bent-over tree with a knife. They watched as he completed the finishing touches on the job, snapped his knife shut and turned to leave with a smug smirk on his face.

"Sorry you guys, but I gotta go teach that kid a quick lesson. Wait here for a second. I'll be right back," Sydney said as she set off after Morton.

"Sydney!" Turk hissed at her.

"What?"

"Leave him alone. If you do anything to him, I swear, I'm going to take off in the other direction and you'll never see me again and I mean it. For real," Turk said.

"Turk, seriously. That kid needs to be taught a lesson and you know it. Don't you remember what he did to Shep's house?"

"For Pete's sake, Sydney. Shep doesn't even remember what he did to Shep's house."

"What Pete did to whose house?" Shep asked.

"See?" Turk said. "Why do you always think you have to go around teaching people lessons? You can't teach a mean kid like that a lesson. It'll just make him meaner. He has to learn his lessons for himself. That's how people learn lessons. It's not your job to do it."

Sydney hesitated, torn between respecting her little brother, and her burning desire to teach Morton a lesson. It was, in fact, no contest. She turned and stood there watching Morton swagger away. It's really too bad that Morton would never know how Turk saved him from another swim in the Rat River that day.

The main reason Morton had come down to the riverbank wasn't to carve initials in the tree. He was there, along with about a hundred other citizens of The Royal Woods, to help tear down and cart away the bird man's shack and, hopefully, to witness the police apprehending Shep, Sydney, and Turk.

There was a tense standoff underway when Morton got to Shep's clearing. The police had the place completely surrounded, and had pushed the crowd well back from the scene. Someone must have forgotten to inform the police that the Bengal tiger on Shep's roof was just a plush toy. Believing it to be real, the police were crouching behind trees with guns drawn.

A police officer was bawling into a bullhorn. "We've got you completely surrounded. Come out of the house with your hands up. Subdue the tiger, or we'll shoot. Surrender immediately!"

Sydney, Turk, and Shep heard what was going on before they saw it. They came around the bend in the trail and edged in at the back of the crowd beside the clearing. Everyone was so fixed on the police operation that no one even noticed their arrival. Wild gusts of wind blasted through the clearing, shaking the trees.

"We can't stick around here," Turk said, tugging at Sydney. Just as they were turning to leave, Bob and Barb Buick and their twin sons Brad and Chad, along with Dee Dee and President Shrub, all came marching up the trail from the other side of the clearing.

"What's the holdup?" Bob Buick fumed. "You fools! It's nothing but a plush toy!" He strode into the clearing and grabbed the tiger roughly by the neck.

And then a most astonishing thing happened. For a split second, the tiger seemed to come to life. The big animal was heard to snarl as it sprang at Bob's head and sent him crashing to the ground. The crowd screamed in horror. Bob wrestled the tiger off and jumped up. The police cocked their guns and aimed them at the tiger. But it only lay there motionless on the ground. It was just a plush toy after all. Who knows what magic power had brought it momentarily to life? Probably it was just the wind that blew the tiger off the shack and sent it flying at Bob. But you'll never convince Sydney and Turk of that. They'll always believe that it was Shep who caused that most astonishing thing to happen.

"Look, everyone!" Dee Dee shrieked. "There they are! And they've got the kidnapped pony!"

The crowd all turned to see Sydney, Turk, Shep, with Janet on the pony, slipping away on the trail. There was a moment of uncertainty, and then the crowd surged toward them, with the police trying to force their way to the front. The officer with the bullhorn yelled, "Stop! Police! You're under arrest!"

Fortunately for our little group, they had a good head start. And since they were all fast runners, and knew the best short cuts on the trails, they were already racing across the mall parking lot before any of their pursuers had even found their way up and out of the trees by the riverbank.

"To the family fun fair!" Sydney shouted against the roaring wind.

By then, Turk realized what Sydney had in mind. Even if he didn't think it was such a great idea, he knew he had no choice about it now. They burst through the gates of the fairgrounds, and pushed through the crowd until they came to the centre of the midway. Shep knew what Sydney had in mind, too. He plucked Janet off the pony's back, and tossed her into the basket of the hot-air balloon.

"Get in!" Sydney yelled. "I'll get the ropes."

Shep climbed into the basket to try to get Janet to settle down, while Turk helped Sydney untie the ropes.

"Now, Turk! Quick! Hop in!" Sydney called, as she untied the last rope.

Turk grabbed onto the side of the basket and was struggling to pull himself up when a sudden blast of wind yanked the balloon into the air with a violent jolt. Turk was thrown off the side of the basket and fell to the ground beside Sydney. He found himself lying flat on his back, looking straight up at the balloon, which by then was as high as a treetop, and rising fast. A crack of thunder and lightning exploded directly above the fairground, like a blast from God's own shotgun. The black sky opened, and hailstones as big as golf balls came crashing down and bounced all around the fairgrounds. Everyone screamed and ran for cover. Sydney pulled Turk to his feet, grabbed the pony's reins, and pushed them both under the roof of a ticket booth.

"This is just like the dream I had!" Turk yelled over the noise of the pounding hailstones and the crashing roar of the thunder.

"Really?" Sydney hollered back.

It reminded Sydney of something too, but she couldn't remember what. She watched the balloon sail off in the wind, as quick as a jet leaving a runway. Shep was in the basket, gesturing grandly as he made a speech to the crowd below. When she caught a word of what Shep was saying, Sydney realized what this reminded her of: *The Wizard of Oz*. Shep was saying farewell to the people of the Emerald City, and entrusting the Tin Man, the Scarecrow and the Cowardly Lion to rule the land of Oz in his absence. Sydney couldn't help but laugh, just before she started to cry. Through tears of laughter, and just plain tears, she watched the balloon zooming southwards over The Royal Woods and beyond, until the smiling face of Bob Buick was just a tiny dot in the sky. Then it disappeared from sight.

CHAPTER THIRTEEN

THE LUCKY PUTTER

Weather changes everything. It's a special power that only the weather has. It can change your mood, alter your plans, and transform your whole day, for better or for worse. Just such a change occurred in The Royal Woods that afternoon. The abrupt change of weather changed everything in an instant. After days of heat and clear blue skies, it was suddenly cold and dark and wet. The hail soon gave way to rain, which lashed the empty fairgrounds in windblown sheets of icy water. When the hail stopped, all the people in the fairgrounds sprinted for their cars in the driving rain and headed for home. The weather seemed to have made them forget all about Sydney, Turk, and Shep. Either that, or the police and the mob from the riverbank must have thought that all three of them had managed to make their escape in the hot-air balloon. Whatever the reason, the chase was abandoned and everyone fled the storm, leaving Sydney and Turk alone in the fairground.

The weather seemed to have brought a change on Sydney, too. For the first time since they'd run away, she was thinking about home. Standing under the roof of the ticket booth with Turk and the little pony, she watched the rain flood the midway, and thought about how nice it would be to talk with her best friends, listen to her favourite songs, and sleep in her own bed in her own little bedroom. Turk was having similar thoughts, although his had begun almost from the moment of their arrival in The Royal Woods.

"What should we do with the pony?" Turk asked.

"I'm so hungry I could probably eat it," Sydney said. "I think I forgot to eat anything today. Anyway, let's just leave it over at the pony ride. That's what Shep wanted to do. Boy, am I ever starving."

Although tempting, Turk was far too considerate to describe the outrageous three-course breakfast he'd enjoyed at the clubhouse that morning.

There was a small shed beside the pony ride, and all the ponies were huddled in there together to keep warm and dry. The little palomino was delighted to finally be home. He trotted into the shed and nuzzled up with his friends.

"What now?" Turk asked. "How about getting something to eat at the mall?"

"Not the mall," Sydney said. "I couldn't cope with that stupid mall. And we'd probably end up getting recognized by someone and then who knows what would happen. Let's go see if Kumar's at the gas bar yet."

"Okay," Turk said. "Good idea."

They trudged across the empty parking lot in the wind and rain. It wasn't worth running to get out of the storm now. They were already soaking wet to the bone, and they couldn't get any more wet even if they tried. The cold was starting to get to them though, especially Sydney, who didn't have the benefit of a big buffet breakfast like Turk. She was hugging herself tightly, and her whole body was trembling in the wet chill. Neither of them was prepared for this kind of weather, since they had both dressed for another hot summer day, in T-shirts and cut-off jean shorts.

"So I finally asked Bob Buick if he knew where Uncle Frank and Aunt Lily went, and you know what he said?" Sydney said through her chattering teeth. "'Don't know, don't care, kid.' And that's it, not another word about it. Just, 'Don't know, don't care, kid.' Oh, I am so glad Shep took off with that guy's balloon."

Sydney could do a perfect impersonation of Bob Buick's plummy radio voice, and she mimicked him all the way across the parking lot to the gas bar, complete with his weird pasted-on smile. She pretended that Bob was trying to sell Shep's shack: "You will just love its rustic rural charm and gorgeous riverfront location. And you and your entire family will enjoy eating out of dumpsters, and hanging out with the millions of friendly mosquitoes who visit there every evening. Yes, Mr. Crabstock, you will live like the king of the hoboes in The Royal Woods."

It made Turk crack up laughing to watch his soaking-wet sister do her impersonation of Bob Buick, all the while shuddering and shaking with cold, and with her lips turning an alarming shade of blue.

But the comedy ended when they got to the gas bar. Kumar wasn't working there, and it looked like he'd never work there again.

"He got fired," the skinny teenaged boy working in the booth told them.

"What for?" Sydney asked.

"He missed a couple of shifts, and then the boss found out he wasn't even supposed to be working here because he's an illegal immigrant. So he fired him. It's too bad. He seemed like an okay guy," the boy said.

"Yeah," Sydney said. "He is an okay guy."

Of all the things that had happened that day, this was the worst yet. Sydney and Turk were stunned by the news. It was especially bad for Sydney, because she had a terrible feeling that she and Turk were in some way responsible for Kumar's troubles. Why had he taken time off work? It wasn't like him. She couldn't help but think that they had something to do with it.

"Wait a minute," Turk said as she turned to leave. "We should at least get something to eat here."

"Yeah," Sydney said, "you're right."

Sydney bought some beef jerky, a big bag of ripple chips, and two cartons of chocolate milk, which she paid for with a ten-dollar bill that was so wet and mashed up it looked like a wad of used chewing gum.

Since they were there anyway, Turk decided to make one more try at phoning their dad. It would be getting toward evening back home, and even if their dad had gone out for the day, he had to be back by now. Sydney hovered around outside the phone booth in the rain, trying to appear as nonchalant as possible.

"Still no answer," Turk said, hanging up the phone. Having been through this a couple of times already, Turk was used to the disappointment, and he greeted it with a resigned sigh.

"Are you sure you did it right?" Sydney asked.

"I think so," Turk said. "You try."

Sydney squeezed into the phone booth beside Turk. She tried, but the result was the same. In typical Sydney fashion though, she didn't just quietly hang up the phone. She slammed the receiver down and said, "Fiddlesticks!" Or a word something like that.

They scrunched down in opposite corners of the phone booth, glad for the chance to get out of the rain for a moment. It was kind of funny to think that, after days of roaming about freely all over The Royal Woods, the only place they felt safe now was the inside of a phone booth. They sat in there eating the food Sydney had bought at the gas bar. Turk couldn't help but recall how much more luxurious and delicious his breakfast had been, although he still didn't mention a word about it to Sydney. Having dined in style at the country club that morning, it was quite a contrast to be squatting in a phone booth, chewing on beef jerky.

"I think we should go back to that house for a little while," Turk said after they'd finished eating.

"What for? And what if Bob Buick comes along and finds us in there?"

"We won't stay long. It'll just take a few minutes."

"What for?" Sydney asked again.

"Well, for one thing, so we can get out of this phone booth. Plus we can stay in the house till we get dry. And also . . . I sort of forgot something there."

The last few words Turk just mumbled.

"What?" Sydney asked. "You what?"

"I forgot my putter," Turk moaned. "That lucky putter that Chip gave me? It's for good luck. I need it."

"Whatever. We might as well go get it then," Sydney said with a shrug. "It's all we got left now anyway. We lost all our stuff at Shep's place. All we got now is, like, about twenty bucks and that stupid putter. Maybe we can sell the thing."

"No way," Turk said.

The long walk to the house was pretty grim. If The Royal Woods could seem bleak and lonely on a sunny summer day, just imagine what it felt like in the pouring rain under a grey wet-blanket sky. Being inside that big empty house wasn't much better. What made it even worse was the fear of getting caught, which really put them on edge. At least the storm had finally passed, and the sky outside was starting to clear.

"I got it," Turk said, coming downstairs with the putter.

"Yippee," Sydney said glumly. "Let's go."

"Go where?" Turk asked.

That was a good question. It felt like they were beginning all over again from the very start, with nothing but a little bit of money and no idea about what to do next.

Because the wind was just right, from off in the distance, Sydney could hear the sound of a train being shunted through the rail yard. The box cars banged, the steel wheels whistled, and the big train horn blasted—long and loud. It seemed to be calling just for them. Sydney realized then what they would have to do.

"Let's go outside and think about it," Sydney said. "We'll think of something. Eventually, I hope."

They went out the front door and sat on the step. From there, with The Royal Woods at their backs, they could enjoy the view of the prairie, and maybe it would give them the courage they'd need to face whatever came next. Or maybe it would just let them pretend, for a little while anyway, that they were back on the farm. The sky was putting on quite a show. The clouds were rolling away to the south, as black as coal and sparking with lightning, and the sky all around them had been washed a crystal clear blue by the storm. To the west, the setting sun turned the horizon a lush orange tinted with rosy pink. Turk counted at least six separate rainbows.

They sat there in silence, just enjoying the show, until Turk said, "What are you thinking about?"

"I'm thinking about how we have to go now," Sydney said.

"Go where?" Turk asked.

Sydney didn't answer at first. She needed to think about that some more. Then she said, "I don't know. We just have to go. We can go anywhere we want. Listen. Hear that train?"

Turk turned his head in the direction of the rail yard. He hadn't noticed it before, but now he could hear the train too, loud and clear. "Where do you think it's going?" he asked.

"Maybe we should find out," Sydney said.

"Okay. But what if it's going east? I mean, like, what if it's headed home?"

Before Sydney could answer, they were distracted by a big white car cruising slowly down the street. The car came to a sudden stop just past the house, and then quickly backed up.

"Oh no," Sydney moaned, "what now?"

Turk was already on his feet, holding his lucky putter, ready to flee in an instant if whoever was in that car came charging out after them. When the car door opened, Sydney jumped up, too. Turk leapt off the step and was turning to run away when a familiar voice called, "Hey! Turk!"

Turk stopped and watched as, one by one, four people he knew got out of the car. First Kumar got out, followed by Uncle Frank and then Aunt Lily. And the last person to get out was me, their dad.

This is where I step out of the car and walk right into the story that I've been telling you all along. Actually, it's the story that Sydney and Turk told me, and then I wrote it all down, thinking it might be interesting for them to read. And hopefully, interesting for you to read, too.

As you can imagine, it was quite an emotional reunion, but complicated as well. Turk was simply overjoyed to see us. There was nothing in the world Turk wanted more than to see the four of us at that very moment. It was well beyond his wildest hopes, and it was almost impossible for him to believe it was true. I can't describe the look of astonishment on Turk's face, as he scrambled around, greeting and hugging each of us one at a time, repeating our names out loud, as if trying to convince himself that it was really true and that it was really us. Sydney, however, was a different matter. I could tell that she was glad to see us too, although she did a pretty good job of hiding it. She didn't like the idea of being rescued by anyone, least of all by me. Of course she was nice and friendly with Kumar, and even more so with Uncle Frank and Aunt Lily. But with me, well, that wasn't going to quite be so easy.

We all piled into the car I'd rented. All except for Sydney, that is. She stood on the street, staring into the distance, watching the storm clouds disappear in the big prairie sky. She seemed undecided about whether to come with us or not. Turk got out of the car and talked to her. I don't know what he said, but I saw them do their secret handshake—two snaps, two slaps and one long palm slide—then they both climbed into the car and we drove away.

If there's a hero in this story, it most certainly has to be Kumar. I have him to thank for helping me find Sydney and Turk. As soon as he learned that they'd run away from home, Kumar went to the local library and searched the names of missing children on the computer. He found Sydney and Turk listed, and then he made contact with me, also on the computer. After we got to know and trust one another, we made a plan for me to come and find Sydney and Turk. Meanwhile, Kumar was to keep a close eye on them. We decided that he shouldn't tell them what was happening, for fear that Sydney would take off and run away even further. That's why, that morning at the dough-nut shop, Kumar had told Turk that he'd had a vision of his dad, and that it wasn't necessary to phone home. Kumar actually did have a vision of me, but it was really just me chatting with him on the computer in the library.

And Sydney was right—all the time Kumar spent deal-ing with this problem had caused him to lose his job. It had also caused him an immense amount of stress and worry, not only about Sydney and Turk, but even more so about his own children, who he'd been missing terribly. That's why, when all of this was over, Kumar went home. He plans to come back though, and this time he'll have the papers he needs to work. Next year, he and his whole fam-ily are planning to return and settle in The Royal Woods. Kumar loves it there.

"It's so clean and orderly," Kumar told me. "Perfect for the raising of a family. And such magnificent facilities! The Royal Woods is truly a paradise on earth."

I didn't have the heart to tell him about the winter.

As for Sydney, well, she can stay mad for a very long time, but she can't stay quiet for more than a few minutes. Soon after we were all back together again, Sydney started talking. And the easiest thing for her to talk about was the story of their adventures. Actually, to me, that was the only thing she was willing to talk about. She started slowly, just mentioning one little detail or another. I was full of questions, and she'd answer them, which led to more details, and so it went, until the whole story unfolded. Of course Turk was also there to contribute his side of things. In fact it was Turk who provided many of the best parts in the story. Before long, I knew the entire saga. And now you do, too.

Did all the things in this story actually happen? You have to decide that for yourself. It's all exactly as they told me, and I prefer to believe that every word is true. Some of it might seem a bit far-fetched to you—two kids riding across the country on a freight train, showering in a car wash, living in vacant houses, and surviving by caddying and hunting for lost golf balls. Maybe they just found a couple of golf balls at the country club one morning, and that's all that really happened there. And maybe Shep McParlain, Jr. was just some crazy homeless guy they met behind the mall, who lived in a cardboard box by the river and liked to whistle a lot. And maybe you find it hard to believe that a chicken can ride a pony, or that a plush Bengal tiger can briefly come to life.

But I will tell you this. A couple of weeks ago, I came across a small article in the newspaper about a man who was travelling around Mexico in a hot-air balloon, putting on performances with a dancing chicken at country fairs and festivals. They call him *"El Hombre-Pajaro Loco del Norte,"* which means the crazy bird man from the north. I think it sounds much better in Spanish, don't you?

Sydney, Turk and I went to stay with Uncle Frank and Aunt Lily at their new place in the country for a few days. It's just a small house at the edge of a little town on the Rat River, many miles south of The Royal Woods. It's not really a farm—they're too old to farm anymore—but they have a little bit of land and a couple of horses, so Sydney and Turk got to do all the things that they'd been dreaming of doing when they first planned their journey. Most of all, they got to visit with Uncle Frank and Aunt Lily, which is what they'd been dreaming of doing most of all. It was the best and happiest time they'd had in years. The funny thing is, I had been planning all along to take Turk and Sydney there for a visit this summer. It was supposed to be a surprise. I guess I should have told them about it before, and then none of this would have happened. Sydney never liked surprises much anyway.

After we said goodbye to Uncle Frank and Aunt Lily, and set off for the long drive home, Turk asked if they could have one last look at The Royal Woods. I was eager to look around there too, just to see all the places that I'd heard so much about. We drove up there and stopped in for doughnuts at the Chubby Princess, and then visited the Rat River Golf and Country Club. Sydney had a long talk with Rene, while Chip Long showed Turk and I around that fabulous country club. It's a shame I didn't have my golf clubs with me.

Then we went for a walk down the riverbank trail. After a long pleasant hike, we came to that old big bent-over tree. To Sydney's horror, Morton had carved the words, "Chad and Sydney—true love" with a big heart around it into the tree trunk.

"So I was wrong," Turk said. "I always thought you were more into Brad."

"As if," Sydney scoffed.

Then we made our way to the clearing where Shep's house used to be. It made them both pretty sad to see the place. There wasn't even one scrap of Shep's house left. Turk searched everywhere, but the only thing he found was a golf ball—that lucky putter still working its magic.

I had a few moments alone with Sydney then. She still wasn't willing to talk to me about much of anything, other than their recent adventures. I didn't mind though. I was so relieved and happy just to have her back with me, I didn't care what Sydney wanted to talk about. And there was still one thing that I needed to know about their story.

"What were you and Turk going to do anyway?" I asked. "I mean, what if we hadn't come along and found you then?"

"I don't know," she said. "We were just going to take off again. We thought you'd gone away and got lost or something. Probably we were just going to keep going west. Or, I don't know. Maybe we were going to come home and try to find you. What do you think we were going to do?"

What I hoped is that they would have come home to find me—that would have been the best part of the whole story, for me anyway. But what I realized was, even though I was there with Sydney, in a way I would never really get her back. At least not the old Sydney I used to know. As I looked at her there—sitting on a stump in the clearing, just gazing out at the trees by the Rat River with her keen green eyes—it struck me that Sydney was a different person now. I hadn't been paying much attention to her since her mom died, so I'd failed to notice how much she'd changed. It's kind of sad for me to say, but I guess I'd lost the old Sydney forever. When I wasn't even looking.

And that's mostly why I wrote all this down. This is from me, for the new Sydney.

Just before we headed out onto the highway for home, we decided to have one final tour of the neighbourhood. They both wanted to see the houses they'd stayed in, and also to pass by the Buicks' place. The problem was, as soon we started driving around in there, I got my directions completely muddled. All the houses looked the same, and the streets all had very similar names. I drove around and around in utter confusion, unable to even figure the way back out.

And just like that, we were lost in The Royal Woods.

MATT DUGGAN was born in Alberta and grew up there and in Manitoba. He has taught high school in Bhutan and Canada, and has written extensively, including several award-winning screenplays, as well as short stories and articles that have appeared in such publications as *Prairie Fire* and *Saturday Night* magazine. He writes and teaches in Toronto, where he lives with his wife and two children. *The Royal Woods* was written for the amusement of his daughter, Mary June, and he is currently working on a novel for adults that she will not be allowed to read.